Bob Moats

I0537504

CRYSTAL PRISON OF KYR

By Bob Moats

Crystal Prison of Kyr

For information and address:
Magic 1 Productions
P.O. Box 524, Fraser MI 48026-0524
Website: http://murdernovels.com

Bob Moats

A Magic 1 Productions Book / published by
arrangement with the author

**Special thanks to Meghan Hyden
(hyde.n.seek.editing@gmail.com)
For finally doing edits for this book.**

"It's never too late to take a chance, it's never too late
to change your life."
Last Chance Harvey

"Fiction is the combination of I remember and let's
pretend."
Berlie Doherty

So, let's pretend. Thanks, Bob Moats.

Crystal Prison of Kyr

By Bob Moats

CHAPTER ONE

JUSTIN WAS HELPLESS on the ground, not able to move a muscle as the dark figure came over him. The sinister being paused a moment, raised its arms toward the boy, and then as the demon's face glowed, radiant energy shot from its hands. Justin could feel his body being enveloped in the painful rays and could feel his soul going numb. As his brain fought the torturous pain, his mind went back to the events of the last week that brought him to this agony. In a small part of his mind, he could see himself sitting safely in his home reviewing his schoolbooks and, for a brief moment, re-lived it.

******

"What are you doing, Cheek?" inquired Justin of his furry friend.

Cheek, a tiny white mouse, looked up from the even tinier piece of paper that he held in his paws and said in a deep voice, "I was studying this note left for me by Edan. It is a new riddle that he sent to challenge me with."

Justin set aside the book he was reading, slid out of the chair and approached the shelf where the red-eyed creature sat engrossed in the piece of parchment. Justin tried to look over the non-existent shoulder of the mouse, but could not read the minuscule writing.

"May I hear what it has to say?" asked Justin, always interested in the battle of wits between Cheek and Edan, the wisest elder of the Myrah Clan.

Cheek looked up at his lifelong companion and shook his head. "Justin, my friend, I have always desired the need for mental stimulation, and between yourself and Edan I have had enough to last many lives. This puzzle has me wondering if Edan may be getting senile." Cheek studied the paper once more and read aloud:

Crystal Prison of Kyr

"It is glass, but it's not, it's water, it's air, five sides to its form but only four will compare. The answer found within to the problem you shall seek, belongs to the gentle one, who will conquer the oblique."

Cheek once again looked toward Justin and sighed, "Maybe I've played this game once too often to be interested in racking my brain on them anymore." He placed the paper in the pocket of his vest and got down off the thread spool he used as a chair.

"It sounds more like a statement, or a warning, than a riddle to me," ventured Justin.

"Whatever it may be," yawned Cheek "it is not going to be solved by me tonight. I desire sleep now and you have lessons in the morning. Extinguish the candles and don't forget to lock the doors."

Justin smiled "I may take a brief walk in the garden before I retire. Sleep well my old friend. I'll be back shortly."

Cheek mumbled something unintelligible and waddled off into the dark of the shelf.

Justin quietly slipped out the door and headed toward the center of town.

The evening air was still, yet there seemed to be a small amount of movement in the trees that lined the path to the garden at the center of the town. Justin approached the entrance and turned toward his favorite thinking spot. He rested on the freshly trimmed grass and wondered who had gardening duty this week. It was the law that every able bodied person shall take turns maintaining the garden and Justin had always enjoyed working around the flowers and trees.

As Justin relaxed, he thought back to when he first met Cheek. Edan, the Elder of the clan, had just returned from a long and perilous journey to a place that he would not reveal, and he had brought back many amazing souvenirs to give to his friends. When it came time to present the five-year-old Justin his present, Edan took the youth aside and handed him a small hole-filled box. Justin opened the box to find a small white mouse inside which Edan explained was a magical mouse that could be taught to speak. Justin smiled as he remembered the long and tedious hours that he spent coaxing the mouse to speak. There were times that he wished he had not, for

Crystal Prison of Kyr

Cheek had become an adopted father to Justin when his real father was killed in the Malvan colonial wars and Cheek took the task too seriously. With Cheek's encouragement, Justin grew into a well-educated youth, and now at twenty-five years old, Justin mentally thanked Edan for his little friend.

A Heram moth flew past Justin's head on its way toward the huge lamp lighting the garden, waking him from his thoughts. Justin had no dislike for the large ugly creature, but would have preferred that it would go elsewhere. As he watched the bat-like beast circling the flames of the lamp, he suddenly felt a shiver run through his body.

The leaves of the trees were turning upwards towards the rising moon in the North, as they always had, but as the moon rose higher, Justin noticed that the familiar blue color had turned to a deep red. This startled Justin, as he had never seen this color before. It seemed as though the light were coming from another source, reflecting off the huge orb. As he watched in fascination, the red hue flickered between yellow and orange reminding Justin of a campfire.

Justin could not move as he watched the moon now overhead. He imagined that he was seeing the reflection of a huge Northworld fire reflecting off the face of the moon, but since he had heard stories that the Northworld was nothing more than ice and many dead stone-cold trees, a fire would be out of the question.

Justin was alone in the garden and he wondered if anyone in town was still awake to witness this phenomenon that surely could not be natural. The moon rose higher in the sky and as it did, the flames faded from its face. Shortly the dancing colors were gone and Justin scolded himself for not waking someone to verify what he had witnessed.

Rising from the grass, he suddenly felt as though someone were watching him from behind. He turned toward the darkness at the outer border of the garden but could not see anyone there. Justin felt that his normally peaceful existence was being touched by unknown forces and he was now feeling quite uneasy.

A night owl screeched from above causing Justin to jump. He decided that it would be a good idea to go home and started for the exit. As he turned the last hedge he stopped, for before him was a cloaked figure. The two stood for an awkward moment before the dark form spoke.

"Are you Justin?" came an unusually squeaky voice from the large, sinister hooded person.

"I am," replied Justin mustering up bravely.

"Mandara wishes to see you," the hood spoke.

Justin had heard of the great magician, but had never seen him, and now for some reason, Mandara was requesting his presence.

"Why does Mandara want to see me?"

"Follow me and find out."

"Isn't it a little late for a visit?"

"Mandara never sleeps."

Holding back an urge to laugh at the hooded figure's high pitched voice, Justin had an image in his mind of a very wide eyed man in need of rest, and asked again, "Why me?"

The hood paused and finally asked, "You have seen the blood on the moon?"

Justin stiffened, "Does Mandara know the significance of this oddity?"

"You'll have your answer shortly. Follow me."

With that, the figure turned to leave, but stumbled off the step and crashed to the ground in a heap. Justin stood there in amazement, as the person in the cloak seemed to be fighting to get out. After a few seconds of rolling on the ground, a boy of about sixteen years pulled his frail body out from under the crumpled cloak. Attached to his legs was a makeshift pair of stilts. He just sat there looking rather embarrassed and annoyed at his blunder.

"All right I'm short, go ahead and laugh," whimpered the boy "everyone else does."

"Why would I do that?" replied Justin kindly "I was quite impressed by your masquerade. You aren't also by chance the great Mandara?"

"At great risk to my life, I would never admit to that."

Justin reached out his hand to the boy and helped him to his feet, which with the stilts brought them both face to face.

"My name is Pectin. I am Mandara's apprentice."

"Honored to meet you Pectin, you already know my name, is there anything else that you know?"

"I know that there is something powerfully wrong. I have never seen Mandara so worried, until this afternoon, and when the moon went red, so did his face. I was told to come to the garden to find you. He knew that you'd be here."

Pectin leaned against the tree and unstrapped a stilt, which left him unbalanced and so he came crashing down around the tree.

Justin went to his aid and asked, "Have you used these things much?"

Pectin ignored the comment and continued "Justin, I think that there is trouble coming.

Mandara has been pouring over his books and consulting with Fog, the smoke spirit, all day. He sat by the window from sundown till moon rise, then he went hysterical. Please Justin, come quickly now or I'll lose my job. I wasted enough time trying to get here in this costume."

"Well Pectin, lead the way to Mandara so we shall get this mystery solved."

Pectin gathered the cloak and stilts and hurried down the path leaving the garden, while Justin followed as fast as he could behind the energetic boy. They left the eastern edge of the city and traveled out the Kayber Road, toward the forbidden forest surrounding the Tarro Mountains, where the magician was reported to have lived. Once into the forest, Justin had no idea where he was going, as no one in the Myra Clan was allowed to venture this far in. He could see the mountain face above the trees and a chill ran through him as they drew closer to the huge grey edifice.

After a while, they came to a mountain wall of stone so smooth that it looked to have been made that way. There was no entrance to be seen and Justin wondered why Pectin stood staring at the wall.

Crystal Prison of Kyr

From behind the wall came a low rumbling and slowly the stone slid upward revealing a hallway leading up into the hill. The two young men entered the opening and made their way up. Occasionally the path turned to the left or right and every so often it forked into other hallways, but Pectin seemed to know the right one to take. After what seemed like hours of walking, Justin noticed a light ahead.

As they came up through the last pathway, Justin could smell a strange musty odor that reminded him of old books. His eyes adjusted to the new lighting conditions in the room and he was surprised to find that he was in a rather large cavern. The furniture and other personal items were set up in the middle of the huge area as though it were a permanent campsite. In the middle of the organized mess was a tall bearded man reading a book held in his shaky hands.

The man paid no attention to the two young men as he paced back and forth. Pectin set his clothing aside and walked toward the man carefully and quietly. Standing just outside the circle of tables holding chemist tubes and bottles, Pectin gave a low cough, but the man did not respond. Pectin moved around the tables, trying to get in sight of the pacing magician, but the man turned every time Pectin stood in front of him. Pectin coughed louder, but still no response. Wearily, Pectin leaned against a table to rest and tilted the top causing the glass bottles to crash to the ground. Mandara slowly looked up from his book, toward the noise, and studied the situation before speaking.

"Pectin, I am not a rich man. If you insist on constantly destroying my equipment, you will need to get a real job to pay for it." Mandara looked over toward Justin, smiled a look of relief and spoke, "Welcome little savior, I have been awaiting your arrival."

The term 'savior' puzzled Justin and he stepped forward toward the magician.

"I am here at your request, Mandara. I am quite puzzled by the events of the night. My quiet world has been shaken and I feel that I am in for more rattling."

Mandara chuckled to himself, and then his face went serious. "I am afraid that you are underestimating your fate. Soon you will be embarking on a long and perilous journey to a land far away. You'll be required to perform feats of courage and daring equal to the great heroes of legend."

He placed the book on a table, came to Justin and led him to a large cauldron bubbling in the middle of the area. A strange glow emitted from the huge pot and Justin stifled from the foul odor. Mandara passed his hands over the surface of the pot and the glowing brew brightened as a strange green smoke formed over the pot.

"Justin, I want you to look deep into Fog, the smoke spirit, and you will learn the reason for your quest."

Justin leaned toward the mist hovering above the pot anticipating a vision of evil and danger, but what he saw was not expected. In the wisps, he could clearly see a young beautiful girl dressed in a gleaming, yellow gown.

He turned to Mandara and asked, "This is my fate? A girl? Not too bad looking, I must say. Is she in danger?"

Mandara smiled, "Justin, my brave friend, she is the reason for your dangerous journey to the land of Kyr."

CHAPTER TWO

JUSTIN opened his eyes and saw the ceiling of his room. He was flat on his back in his own bed and he lay there wondering if he had dreamt the events of the night. He remembered being told by Mandara to go home and rest and all would be explained to him the following night. Justin tried to pry more about the girl out of the magician, but Mandara had turned and headed off into the darkness of the cavern. Pectin was unable to provide any more information than what had already transpired, so Justin quietly followed him back to the edge of the city where they parted as friends. Justin slipped quietly into his home, careful not to awaken Cheek, who surely would have interrogated him till dawn. The last thing he recalled was lying on his bed, his head filled with visions of the mystery girl. It was the last image he had before he fell asleep.

Crystal Prison of Kyr

It was also the first image he saw as he awoke that morning. He sat up and looked around for the room seemed unusually quiet. Cheek was normally scurrying around preparing to get Justin off to his agriculture classes, but he was nowhere to be seen. Justin went to Cheek's shelf, but the mouse was not there. He started to worry a little, for his tiny friend would never go out without letting him know.

Justin opened the front door and stepped out into the sunshine. A cold breeze mussed his hair and sent him back in for his coat. Just as he reached the coat rack, he heard a noise at the door, and hoping it to be Cheek, flung it open only to find no one there. As he turned to re-enter, he noticed a note stuck into the cracks of the door. He pulled the paper out and took it to a candle on the table to read.

It was from Edan requesting Justin to come meet him in the garden. Edan was the wisest of the Myrah clan and Justin was sure that he would have some answers to his questions.

As Justin made his way down the narrow roadway toward the garden, he felt a strange eeriness in the now unusually deserted town. A sort of strange silence smothered the air and made the skin on Justin's neck tingle.

As he approached the entrance to the garden, he wished that he didn't have to go in alone. He wished he knew where Cheek was since he could have used some words of wisdom right now. He had never been afraid of Edan, but had a great deal of respect for the man. Since Edan was very reclusive, he usually communicated only through notes and letters. Very few people had come in direct contact with him, and now Justin was going to meet him in the garden of all places.

The sun was almost directly overhead as Justin wrestled with his feelings about all the commotion that had entered his life since the last evening. He wondered why he was becoming involved in the great mystery of the crimson moon and the beautiful girl, so he figured that he might as well face Edan and hopefully get some answers.

Justin took in a breath and entered the garden. Since he had no idea as to where he would find Edan, he figured if he walked around long enough he'd find him. As Justin turned a corner by a tall hedge, he just about had a heart attack, for there was Edan standing there on front of him.

"Welcome Justin, I'm glad you're prompt. Come, we have much to discuss." With that, he turned toward the center of the garden and hurried away leaving Justin paces behind.

By the time Justin caught up with him, Edan was already seated on a bench by the pond. Justin stood for a few moments before Edan motioned to him to sit.

"Justin, right now you know nothing of what is happening to you and unfortunately I cannot tell you more."

Justin's heart sunk and Edan could see this. "I'm sorry Justin, I am bound by oath not to say anything about the land of Kyr and what awaits you there. I can say that I have been there and have gone through the same thing that you will experience."

Justin looked to the old man in surprise, "Edan, you know what is going on with the moon and the girl and yet you can't tell me about it?"

"It seems to me Justin, that I just said that. Please pay closer attention to me, I have a lot of nothing to say before you go to see Mandara."

Embarrassed by his comment, Justin sat in silence as the Elder continued, "I was a young man like you when the moon went red and Mandara summoned me to his cavern and issued to me the challenge of Kyr. You are not obligated to accept the challenge, but I told Mandara that I felt you were the one person who could carry out the task."

Now Justin knew why he was involved in the mystery and felt a sense of honor that the Elder had recommended him.

"I have to warn you Justin, this is a very dangerous task and you will be faced with death often. I don't want anything to happen to you because I like you, but if someone doesn't go to Kyr, the rest of the world will surely die, all humans, animals and plants."

Justin felt a chill run through his body thinking that the fate of everything would depend on him. He never really had a lot of confidence in himself when it came to everyday decisions, so this would really put him to the test.

Edan could see the anxiety in the young man's face. He put his arm around his shoulders and said gently, "Justin, I have been there and while it is dangerous, I have every confidence that you will return safely and unharmed so please set your mind to the task ahead of you."

Justin felt a fatherly warmth in the elder's voice and it helped to relieve the tenseness in his body.

"Edan, what is happening?"

"Well Justin, I am allowed to tell you a few details about the origin of the land of Kyr." Edan paused and looked wistfully into the reflecting pond. "It was nine centuries ago when the last two of the great magicians locked in battle over good and evil. The unusual thing about it all was that it was only one magician battling his alter ego. It was Mandara."

Justin looked in shock at Edan, as he couldn't believe that Mandara was over nine hundred years old.

"Yes Justin, Mandara is now just short of 1200 years old. At one time there were about a hundred or so legitimate magicians on this planet. Most of them discovered that with power comes corruption. Mandara was the leader of a small group that advocated using magic for good purposes throughout the universe. He felt that magicians should be sent out to the backward planets and help the inhabitants there to develop into worthwhile civilizations. The corrupt factions wanted to rule these planets and enslave the life forms for their own enjoyment. Mandara tried to stop them from carrying out their plan but he was out voted by the evil faction. Therefore, Mandara and a small group of fourteen followers decided to meet in secret and plot to stop them. Unknown to Mandara, one of his followers turned the small group in, and on the night they met, the evil group raided the gathering. A battle of magic powers ensued and lasted for hours until only Mandara and the leader of the evil group, were left standing. The evil one was named Kyr and he, unfortunately, was Mandara's twin brother. When they were born, they were joined together at the head, and after they were separated, it seemed that Kyr had retained the evil part of the mind and Mandara the good. Mandara and Kyr had magical powers that were equal in strength, which meant they could not magically outdo each other. Mandara could not, out of goodness, kill his brother, so he tricked him and managed to imprison Kyr in a solid block of ice preventing him from moving. He sent it to the north land, which at one time was a beautiful forest area. In order to prevent anyone from freeing Kyr, Mandara froze the land and booby trapped the surrounding area with all forms of death and terror." Edan looked out over the pond as though he were recalling something that bothered him.

He continued, "Unknown to Mandara, when the entire group of magicians had been killed, the power that they thought they had individually was diminished. It turned out that they fed off each other, and without the group, Mandara and Kyr had only a small portion of the power left. With Kyr imprisoned, Mandara was almost, but not entirely, powerless. Every fifty years or so Mandara's powers go into a sort of recharging and he cannot maintain his hold over Kyr. When the moon glows red, it is a sign that Kyr's powers are growing over Mandara's."

Edan paused a moment, giving Justin time to ask, "If Mandara's powers are weak now, what about Kyr's?"

"Good question Justin, and I'm afraid that no one is really sure whether Kyr's powers are stronger being as he hasn't been able to use them for centuries. The main concern is that he will soon have the opportunity to free himself and possibly wreak havoc on the world."

"But Edan, I thought that without the other magicians around to strengthen him, wouldn't his powers be minor?"

"As a group they were invincible, all powerful. They could move planets and darken suns, so even one of them would have enough power to make life miserable for everyone and everything on our world. Mandara's powers over the ages have been devoted to holding the land of Kyr in its frozen state, which is why he hides in the great cavern focusing his attentions to his evil half. Now that he is temporarily weakening, Kyr will have enough time to escape and overpower him, which is where you will come in."

Panic tightened in Justin's chest as he realized that he was being asked to prevent a powerful evil from destroying everything he loved.

25

Crystal Prison of Kyr

"Isn't there any way to destroy Kyr so he won't be a menace to our world?" inquired Justin, hoping to find a way out of a situation that he felt unable to handle.

"Sorry Justin, but the only way a magician can be destroyed is by another magician. Mandara is the last and he will never do bodily harm to his brother. Mandara has agonized over the problem, and since no harm can come to Mandara, this situation may go on forever. I've noticed a great strain on him in the last few years." Edan's face became sullen.

Justin was feeling a slight strain on himself, but did not want Edan to notice. He was getting very anxious to know what his fate was to be, and since Edan was not going to yield any of the gory details, he couldn't wait to visit Mandara again.

Edan returned from his deep thoughts, looked to the noticeably worried boy, and smiled. Edan thought back to what seemed lifetimes ago when Doran, the Elder of his youth, tried to comfort him prior to his journey to Kyr. Edan knew what was ahead for Justin, but was bound by his oath not to say anything. He knew that only a human, who was unspoiled by evil or corruption, with no knowledge of the deadly dangers ahead, would stand a far better chance of getting through safely to Kyr. Mandara had safeguarded Kyr's imprisonment by casting an irreversible spell in which any human having any knowledge of the traps would automatically fail to get through, and this included Mandara.

"Justin, I have complete faith in you that you will be able to handle the task given to you. I wish I could say more, but I don't want to jeopardize your chances of returning. I won't say that it will be easy, because it's not, but I would not have recommended you if I didn't feel that you were the one to succeed." Edan knew that no further words would ease the tension and anxiety in the boy, and could think of nothing more to say.

Justin comforted the elder man by replying, "Edan, it is a great honor that you have given me. I will not disappoint you by backing down. I will take this one-step at a time and try to think with a clear head. You won't regret your decision to recommend me to Mandara."

The old man felt a new closeness to the boy and put his arm again around Justin's shoulders. The two of them sat there not knowing what more to say, so they spoke to each other with their silence.

After a while, Edan announced that it was time that he returned to his duties and wished Justin well. He told Justin to remain a while in the garden, and left as quickly and quietly as he had come, leaving Justin feeling more alone than he had ever felt before. He sat there sorting the events in his mind when he heard a noise from behind him. Turning, he found the noise to be Pectin. The small boy looked serious and spoke, "Mandara will see you now."

CHAPTER THREE

THE TWO YOUTHS made the journey in silence and Justin tried hard to remember any of the pathways from his last visit to Mandara's cavern, but none of the directions that Pectin took were familiar to him. He wondered if Pectin were taking a different route so that he could not find his way back again and since members of the clan were forbidden to enter this mountain range, Justin still had no idea of where he was. His thoughts were interrupted by the sight of the smooth wall ahead. They entered the opening and he was sure they took a totally different way into the cavern than before. Justin mentally noted to commend Pectin for his care in the security of Mandara's hideaway. They finally entered the great cavern, and when Justin's eyes adjusted to the lighting, he saw that Mandara was nowhere in the room. Pectin finally broke the silence.

"Mandara will be with you shortly." After mumbling these words, Pectin ran off into the dark reaches of the cavern.

Justin wandered over to the circle of tables and felt a shiver run through his body as he entered the circle. The cauldron, in which he first saw the beautiful girl, sat bubbling furiously before him. He wished he knew how to summon Fog, the smoke spirit, so he could see her again, but figured all would come together soon enough.

After what seemed an hour of waiting, Justin started to pace nervously. What was Mandara up to? Was this part of the task ahead, to see if he could stand the pressure?

Crystal Prison of Kyr

Justin was just on the verge of yelling out to see if anyone would answer, when he heard someone approaching from the dark. Justin felt the blood pumping in his veins and thought his heart would explode as he walked cautiously toward the approaching sound, stopping short of the circle of tables. Mandara suddenly appeared out of the darkness before Justin. His face was grave and pale, looking every one of his twelve hundred years. Mandara said nothing as he walked past Justin on his way to the cauldron. The magician stood gazing into the mist rising from the huge kettle and looked as though he were going to cry.

"Justin," he spoke softly, "since the demise of my fellow magicians, I am as close to being a mortal than I could ever have known. It takes all of my energy to hold my brother in his imprisonment, and like humans, I need rest from time to time. At first I rested every hundred years, but the moon turned red about fifty years too early. It's getting harder to use my energy, since I am very old and tired, more tired than I have ever felt."

The magician turned toward Justin. There were small tears forming in the corner of his eyes and he looked more worn out than any man Justin had known. Mandara came to Justin and put his hand on the young man's shoulder.

"Justin, for my own sanity, this must end. I have wasted most of my life hiding here on a truly pointless mission. Out of respect for my brother, I have done him no harm. But if you were totally paralyzed, not being able to move, speak or touch, wouldn't you prefer death? I have killed my brother even though he remains alive, frozen in time. I can imagine the hate he must feel for me, and even though he is evil incarnate, I feel grief for him."

Mandara again turned to the cauldron and continued.

"Justin, eight brave men have gone before you to stop Kyr from escaping and their task was dangerous, and although you are younger than the others, your task is no less dangerous."

Justin felt his spine tingle and his knees began to rattle. Sweat formed on the back of his neck and his palms, and he felt a lump choking his throat.

Crystal Prison of Kyr

"Justin, you have to accept this challenge voluntarily or you will fail from the start. If someone does not stop Kyr, this world will be a desolate place. You must go willingly or not at all."

He looked back at Justin and gave a faint smile. Justin looked into the old man's eyes and saw the agony of his pain. He saw the years of emptiness and solitude that the magician had endured being shut away from the world that he had been protecting all of this time.

A great change came over Justin as he realized that he could make a sacrifice in his comfortable little life to help those in need. He worried so much about the uncertainty and danger of the journey to Kyr, that he forgot about the uncertainty and danger that he faced in his everyday life. That never stopped him from leaving his house, so why should he turn down helping his world and saving this man from a slow, lonely death. Justin felt pride building up in himself and knew that it was time to take responsibility for his life.

"Mandara, I feel the pain in your words and realize the danger to our world. I will take on the quest freely and relieve you of your burden.

I hope that I will be worthy or your confidence," Justin said bravely.

A smile came to Mandara's face and he seemed younger as he replied.

"Spoken like a true hero Justin. Edan chose well in you, and I know now that you will be the savior who will go and conquer the evil endangering our existence and, as I said, my sanity. Thank you Justin."

Mandara embraced him and gave a sigh of relief. He released Justin and turned toward the cauldron, raised his hands over the boiling vapors, and spoke in a language that was unfamiliar to Justin. Mandara's voice grew louder and reverberated throughout the cavern as the bubbling mixture glowed a bright lime color and a heavy mist formed over it.

After a moment of silence from Mandara, he turned to Justin and asked, "Well, my young hero, are you ready to learn about your adventure?"

Justin felt a slight shiver, but stood firm and replied, "As ready as I shall ever be."

Crystal Prison of Kyr

"Good, then look deep into Fog and see your fate."

Justin moved to the cauldron and stared into the haze. He saw many colors swirling and forming into images of long ago. He saw the original coven of magicians, lead by Kyr, and the peaceful faction lead by a youthful Mandara. He witnessed the battle of magical powers, finishing with the standoff between Kyr and Mandara. The image faded before Justin witnessed Kyr's imprisonment, and Mandara explained that he could not see any more as it would jeopardized his quest. The mist swirled back into a kaleidoscope of colors and Justin found himself back in the great cavern. He turned toward Mandara with a new understanding of the powers that had nearly destroyed the universe so many years ago. The threat that Kyr had posed in this present world was now evident to the importance of the quest.

"Mandara, when must I start and how long do I have to complete my task?" inquired Justin bravely.

"When the moon glows red, there is a cycle of one moon to complete the task. The next full moon must rise normally as it has every cycle.

Edan managed to do the job in twenty-two days, far faster than his predecessors, who all just barely completed their goal. Had me worried, I must say. You do have the advantage of youth on your side. The others were much older in their times including Edan. It was Edan's sole responsibility to choose the next person to go, as he knows what is ahead, and has decided that you are the one to handle the situation. I have to put all my trust in his judgment and all my faith in you."

Mandara paused to let everything sink into the youth. Justin looked back to the mist, hoping to catch a glimpse of what was ahead, but knowing he could not.

"Mandara, what of the girl that I saw on my last visit here? How does she fit into all of this?"

Mandara smiled and seemed to hesitate at the question posed by the anxious young man. The old magician felt a bit embarrassed that he had used the vision of the girl as an extra incentive for Justin.

"Justin, the young lady that you witnessed in the smoke was a shadow of things to come. She is someone who you will meet in the near future, if our world is not destroyed. I cannot tell you more about her until you return from your journey."

Justin was feeling very mixed and annoyed by all the secrecy involving his fate. He was still a young man and not experienced with women, or danger, and now he was being asked to deal with both and had no idea what to do with either. Mandara could sense the boy's tension and went to a tall shelf by the opening of the circle. He removed a sack from the shelf and brought it to a table by Justin.

"Come here Justin, I have something for you." Justin approached Mandara and watched the man remove a dark blue cloak from the sack. Mandara placed it around Justin's shoulders and continued, "Justin, this cloak shall protect you from the harmful cold of the Northland. Unfortunately, it will not protect you from harm. I was a little carried away by my spell to prevent my brother from having outside help. I prevented even myself from going there, with what I know of it, and you must have no knowledge of what is ahead or you will never make it alive. No human knows the danger ahead and succeeds."

Justin felt warm in the cloak and was feeling ready to get the deed done and over. The thoughts of the girl helped his enthusiasm. Mandara strode to the opening of the circle and turned, "Justin, you are now to go home and wait for your guide. Good fates be with you as my fate will be in your hands." He turned and disappeared into the darkness. Justin stood there for a brief moment when Pectin startled him from behind and said to follow him.

They parted again at the edge of the city and Justin returned to his home. The house was again empty and Justin was starting to worry about Cheek. His little friend had never been gone this long and had left no notes as to where he was. Justin was tired and sat in the chair that he studied his lessons in. It was the one restful place where he could easily think. He sat there for what seemed hours, and as he was deep in thought, he heard a voice from his right. He turned his head to see Cheek standing on the table. He was dress in an odd-looking coat and he wasn't alone. Next to him was a smaller black mouse wearing a similar coat.

Before Justin could speak, Cheek said in a solemn voice, "Justin, it is time for you to go."

CHAPTER FOUR

JUSTIN JUMPED from his chair and knelt at the table, putting his face just inches from his furry friend. "Cheek where have you been and have I got a story to tell you!"

Cheek approached Justin and smacked him on the nose with his tiny paw. "Justin, you will have to learn to let your elders speak first. I know the story you are bursting to tell because Edan has told me of your forthcoming ordeal. He has given me the task of getting you to the Northland without losing your way. My new friend here, Kigamsti, knows the fastest route and has agreed to get us there. I hope you have prepared by packing some food and a change of clothes?"

Justin felt a little embarrassed that he had not. He ran to his room, packed a backpack with clothes, and then to the pantry for food. Cheek sat conversing with the dark rodent as though they were plotting something.

Bob Moats

"I am ready, Cheek. When do we start?"

Cheek and Kigamsti came to the edge of the table and Justin bent down to allow them to climb into his coat pocket.

"Well, Justin the first thing we must do is go out the door or the journey won't begin." Cheek commanded "And don't forget to lock up."

They headed out the north road riding Justin's favorite horse, Canter. The groom had Canter saddled for him, as though he knew the horse would be needed. Edan must be behind much the preparations, Justin thought.

"Justin, keep on this road till it breaks to the right and follow the left path," Cheek shouted from the pocket. Justin could hear the two mice chattering in his pocket, and was sorry that the dark mouse could not speak human for he would have liked to know what they were saying.

They rode until dark on the twisting paths and roads as directed by Kigamsti through Cheek. Finally, it was too dark to venture further and Cheek said to stop and bed down for the night.

Crystal Prison of Kyr

As they sat by the fire, Justin looked over to where the two mice were sitting on the backpack, both just staring quietly into the fire. Their eyes glowed red from the bright flames of the fire, making the two of them look menacing. Justin knew that his friend would never hurt him or anyone else, but at that moment, he looked as though he could deal with any enemy to come along. The dark mouse looked like he came off one of the rough sailing vessels that brought goods from faraway lands. Justin felt that he could trust this strange creature, for Cheek would have never asked for his help otherwise.

Justin laid back and decided that sleep would be the best for him right now, as they had a long journey ahead. While Justin drifted into sleep, the two mice quietly started chattering and watched the fire. Cheek had cared so much for Justin that no amount of careful planning would be enough to take care of his safety.

The morning sun came brightly and they prepared to leave.

"How long will it take us to get to the Northlands, Cheek?" inquired Justin.

"About five days of uninterrupted travel and I hope that we are not interrupted," he said cautiously.

"What do you mean by that Cheek?" asked Justin, wondering about the comment.

"We will be traveling through some pretty rough towns and I would prefer that we could avoid them altogether."

"We'll deal with that when we get to it," comforted Justin. They were packed and ready to go, so Justin carefully loaded his tiny passengers into his pocket, mounted the horse and headed up the path to the road continuing northward.

Justin had never been this far north and the beauty of the countryside was overwhelming. As they journeyed further, the land became more mountainous and the road was quickly becoming a trail. They had passed through a few small towns and at Cheek's insistence, they passed through them without stopping. Cheek said that there would be plenty of time later to sightsee. Cheek and Kigamsti were still squeaking to each other, and Justin was getting to the point of reminding Cheek that it was not polite to converse when he couldn't understand them, but decided not to.

Finally, the sun was very low on the horizon and the looming mountains made it seem darker. Justin called to Cheek in his pocket and the mouse peeked out and said that it would be a good time to rest for the night. Wearily, Justin made camp and the tired group stretched out before the fire.

Justin was quite worn out by the ride and bored by having no one to talk to. Cheek had been so busy conversing with Kigamsti that he neglected Justin, but since Cheek seemed happy to have someone of his own species to talk to, Justin didn't mind. Besides, it gave him time to think about what was happening and more so, about the girl in the mist. Was she a lonely princess in need of rescue or perhaps a vision of his future bride? Only Mandara knew and he wasn't saying anything until Justin proved himself by safely returning home.

Justin's thoughts were interrupted by a crackling noise to his left. It sounded as though someone were approaching and Justin had no idea what kind of human or creature would be out wandering at this late hour. Cheek poked his head out of the backpack for he also had heard the noise.

"Justin," Cheek whispered, "Do you have your sword handy?"

"Yes, I have it," quietly replied Justin. "What do you think it is?"

"We'll both know when it gets here. I hope you paid attention to all the sword training you had at school."

Justin was already up and crouching low with sword in hand, focusing his attention to the area of the sound. It grew louder and sounded as though a clumsy bear were lost in the dark. Justin moved around to put the fire between him and the noise. Cheek and Kigamsti vacated the backpack and found a burrow to crawl into. The noise grew louder and Justin tensed as a shape came through the brush, stumbled and fell before the fire pit. It was Pectin.

"Pectin! What are you doing here?" demanded Justin.

"Don't hurt me, sir! I have been trying to find you since you left. My horse threw me and ran off on the trail and I have been on foot since yesterday." Pectin shivered and moved to the fire to warm.

"When everyone left I was going crazy with worry and decided that I wanted to come help you save our world. If you permit me to."

Justin didn't know what to say. The boy looked so sincere that he didn't want to turn him back, but was not sure if Pectin could accompany him to Kyr. Cheek and Kigamsti were chattering at the opening of the burrow. Justin moved over to them hoping Cheek may have had some instructions from Edan that may help decide the fate of the young apprentice.

"Cheek, I don't know what to say to him. Can we take him along or will it jeopardize our chances?" Justin asked hoping his wise friend would have an answer.

"Well, if the young, clumsy fool doesn't care if he is killed and doesn't get in the way, he may come." Cheek turned to Pectin and asked "Pectin, you must swear to us that you have no knowledge of what is ahead and have not overheard Mandara speaking of it."

"Master Cheek, I know no more than Justin does. I have been a failure as Mandara's apprentice and I hope to prove to him that I can be good for something," Pectin replied honestly.

Kigamsti said something to Cheek, who in turn asked Pectin "Does Mandara know that you are here?"

"I left him a note, so he probably knows by now. I hope I haven't angered him, but I had to do this."

"Well, Pectin, your help is welcome, but stay out of the way until you are needed or you will be sent back to face Mandara," Cheek ordered. "Justin, Kigamsti tells me there is a town down this road in the valley before the hills of the Northland. There we can replace the horse that Pectin lost. Now, I think that since it is almost daylight, we may as well use this time to do so.' Cheek and Kigamsti scurried to the backpack while Justin helped Pectin to his feet.

"Well my friend, may the fates be on our side, we will need it," Justin said with a smile and the two young men broke camp.

Crystal Prison of Kyr

On the road, Pectin ran to keep up with the horse, too loaded down with Justin and the packs to allow Pectin to ride. The town was not far and there they would hopefully find a horse for him. Cheek did not want to stop at the town but this one time would be necessary.

They had just peaked the last hill before the town, settled down in the valley. The small scattering of buildings didn't suggest much of a community, but Justin hoped they would be able to find a horse there. Beyond the town, a road led to the beginning of the crystal white hills of the Northland and Justin could feel the chill, both from the cold and from what lay ahead.

They headed down into the valley and approached the south gate of the town. There were a few people milling around in the streets, but it seemed more deserted than most of the small villages they had gone through.

"Cheek, I think that you and Kigamsti had better stay hidden. I don't know if these people would take to a talking mouse," Justin warned his friend.

"My feelings exactly, Justin. Be very careful here. These people know of the evil of

Kyr and don't trust outsiders. They have had renegades come through in hopes of freeing Kyr, although none have ever returned from the frozen north."

Justin hoped that his mission would be better received by the townspeople but with the threat hanging over them, he wouldn't blame them if they didn't trust him. A freed Kyr would devastate their town first on his way out.

They passed through the south gate without any problems and receive a few dark stares from the men gathered in front of the tiny tavern. The five men turned toward Justin and Pectin as they approached and didn't act too friendly as Justin asked if they had a stable.

"Who wants to know and what's your business here?" inquired the biggest, dirtiest of the men.

"I am Justin of Freland with my assistant, Pectin. We are on a mission for the great Mandara, and we need a horse, if there is one to spare."

The men laughed and just stood looking Justin over.

"Maybe they're not smart enough to understand the question," mumbled Pectin.

The big man growled under his breath and said, "So the little boy thinks he can speak for his master, who is just another little boy. We love to feed little boys to the Northland. Are you brave enough, little boy?"

"I'm brave enough to have volunteered to go there and stop Kyr!" boldly spoke Pectin, waiting to be smashed by the brute.

"That's enough, Pectin!" ordered Justin. "Our mission is none of their business."

The big man studied Pectin closely and said, "The moon has shown red and two boy strangers appear at our gates. If Mandara has sent you, he is getting senile. Do you young fools think you can stop Kyr? Do you know what you're up against? The biggest and meanest of men and warriors have passed here to free Kyr for their own gain and never came back. But we have heard their screams from over the crystal hills, and we weren't fools enough to go help them. Yes, Mandara has sent brave men to stop Kyr during the red moon and they have returned, keeping our lands and souls safe. But they were brave men, not puny little boys." The man turned to his friends and continued, "Well, we may as well go dig our graves, for we are surely doomed."

"Dig if you will, but you'll be planting vegetables and not bodies," spoke out Justin. "But since you know that all is lost, then you won't miss one little horse or don't you have any."

The man looked up at Justin and fell silent. He turned to his companions and said something to the nearest man. The man ran off around the building and the big man turned toward Justin.

"We will give you our best animal and expect it to be returned on your way back, if you come back." he sneered sarcastically. The other man came around the building pulling at a very run down looking mule who seemed to want to go elsewhere.

"This is the best you have, an old mule?" demanded Justin.

"Yes!" hissed the man. "All our good horses were taken by the idiots who went to their deaths." He then looked like he was giving up. "I fear this is the last time we will have to worry about anyone coming through here again." He walked toward the tavern. "As for me, I'm going to drink until it's over. I don't want to face Kyr while I'm sober." He went in, followed by the other men.

Justin knew nothing he could say would make any difference to the men, so he told Pectin to mount the mule and follow. As they headed out the road toward the crystal hills, the big man stood on the steps of the tavern with bottle in hand. He held it high in salute to them, and softly said, "May the Fates be with you, little boys."

CHAPTER FIVE

THE RIDE to the crystal hills went without talk. Pectin finally got the mule to cooperate and he followed the horse as fast as the bowlegged beast could move. Occasionally

Justin had to stop to allow Pectin to catch up and Cheek would complain every time he did so.

"Oh Cheek, must you be so hard on him. He has a real desire to help and we may need him," scolded Justin.

"If we don't keep up with the schedule, we may not make it in time to need his help," grumbled Cheek and then went back to converse with his companion.

The road started to climb upward and was starting to turn white. The land was completely made up of the remains of a once living forestland now covered in ice crystals, some crystals standing twice as high as Justin and his horse. The sunlight beamed through the crystals creating a rainbow of colors everywhere and Justin felt he was in a fantasyland where nothing seemed real. The cold air was kept away by the cloak that Mandara had given him. Pectin, at least, had thought to bring a warm coat, and the mice were protected by their strange little jackets, probably given to them by Edan.

They had just come around a bend in the road and found that they were surrounded by huge crystal walls on both sides of them. This made Justin a little nervous, as there were only two ways to go, forward or back, so it would be a bad time to run into danger here.

They traveled on and the road angled down, twisting and turning haphazardly. They were coming to a sharp climb, when they heard a mournful howling sound ahead, so Justin stopped the horse and listened.

"What was that?" cried Pectin from behind.

"Quiet Pectin and listen," cautioned Justin. He cocked his head and heard nothing. After a moment, he coaxed the horse forward, but found that Canter would not budge. His heels jabbed the horse but once again, the horse refused to move.

"What is the matter now?" moaned Cheek, poking his head out of the pocket.

"I just heard a strange sound and now Canter won't move," answered Justin.

Cheek was just about to ask what sound when a huge shape came up over the small hill. It was a snakelike beast on short legs with large paws. Its head was jagged and frosty white, as was its body, and again it made the howling that Justin had heard moments before. It definitely was not acting friendly as it came over the hill toward them. The horse and mule panicked, throwing their riders to the ground and bolted back down the road. Justin had no time to get to his sword for the beast was almost on top of him. He quickly rolled to the side of the road, just as the creature stomped its large paw down where Justin had been. Pectin was already on his feet and was racing toward a break in the crystal wall. Justin rolled again avoiding the stomping beast, and then finally managed to get to his feet as he spied the crack hiding the now ash-white faced Pectin. He ran and dove in just as the monster's tail crashed into the crystal wall barely missing Justin by inches.

"Cheek, are you all right?" cried Justin into his pocket.

"Shaken, but alive. What is going on out there?" He poked his head out and saw the monster pacing before the wall opening, howling at the top of his lungs. He looked up at Justin and said, "Let me know when it's over," and disappeared back into the pocket.

"Thanks Cheek, what am I supposed to do?" Justin wailed.

"Keep your head low," came a voice from the pocket.

Justin heard a strange noise from outside and realized that it was not the beast, but more human sounding. The creature stopped pacing and listened. The sound seemed to come from above the wall behind the monster. As the beast was standing up to better see the origin of the yelling, a great avalanche of crystals came tumbling down crushing the beast beneath the shimmering gems.

It was quiet after a moment and Justin could see no life from the mound of ice, so he slowly moved toward the opening and looked out. It was still silent as he moved out into the open, when an unnerving cry came from above and Justin fell back against the icy wall. He looked up and couldn't believe his eyes, it was the big man from the town. He was whooping and hollering at his success in stopping the beast, then paused and called down. "Is everyone all right down there?"

Justin yelled up that all were still alive and asked what he was doing there.

"I got to thinking that if I'm going to die, I may as well go down fighting while there is still a chance. Wait there, I'll come down." He disappeared past the cliff and Justin helped Pectin out of the hole. They were gathering the packs that fell off the horse as the man came running up the road toward then. He seemed awful happy for a man walking through the land of death.

"Did you see the look of surprise on that beast's face when I pushed the ice down to hit him. He barely saw it coming, I loved it!" He was dancing around enjoying his victory.

"Thank you, friend," said Justin and held out his hand.

"The name is Garth and you're welcome," smiled their new companion. "I'd better see if I can find the horse before it gets eaten by some other monster. I'll run down the road to see if I can catch them."

He took off leaving the shaken boy in a daze. Pectin came up behind him putting his hand on Justin's shoulder causing Justin to jump out of his skin.

"Don't come up behind me like that again if you want to live," breathed Justin.

"I hope there are no more monsters lurking about," Pectin lamented.

"It's just beginning," Cheek reported as he and Kigamsti poked out of the pocket.

"That's comforting to know," sighed Justin. "Pectin, go down the road and see if you can help Garth find the animals, I'll pick up the packs."

Pectin ran off as Justin gathered the scattered packs dropped by the frightened horse. After a while, Cheek popped his head out from the pocket to see what the boy was up to and if the others had come back yet.

"Justin, I don't know if we should trust this Garth. He may be trouble."

"Well, my friend, I feel that there is safety in numbers and if he hadn't killed that beast, we wouldn't be here now," reminded Justin to the skeptical mouse.

"That is true, but I still don't trust him," replied Cheek. "We have still a ways to go before you face Kyr."

"I wish I knew what more dangers lay ahead," said Justin to the tiny mouse.

"That's one wish you don't want to come true," answered Cheek. "It could mean your life and the failure of our quest."

As they stood there talking, a noise came from behind them and Justin turned to see Garth and Pectin coming up the road with the horse and the mule.

"Canter!" cried Justin as he ran to meet them. "You coward, how could you drop me and run like that?"

"I would have done the same if that creature had jumped up in front of me," laughed Garth. "We found them in a small boxed area down trail and they couldn't figure how to get out without coming back this way. If they hadn't gone in there, they probably would have been back to Freland by now."

Justin smiled and felt relief that Garth was there. "Thank you my friend. You have save our lives and I won't forget it."

"Hey, I just wanted to make sure you little boys didn't get hurt before Kyr kills you," smirked Garth. "Besides, everyone in town was in hiding and it was getting boring there, so I've been running along behind you to make sure you stayed out of trouble. Besides I thought I'd like to take a sight-see here in this cursed land."

"If we don't stop gabbing and get moving it will be the last sight we ever see," demanded Cheek.

Garth's eyes went wide as he saw the mouse looking at him from the pocket.

"Fates preserve us! It talked! What mysticism is this?"

Justin smiled and brought Cheek out on the palm of his hand. "Garth, meet my lifelong friend and teacher, Cheek."

Garth moved his head closer to the tiny creature. "Well bless me, a talking rat."

"I am not a rat, you foul smelling oaf! I'm a mouse and proud of it!" Cheek yelled at the face before him.

Garth jumped back in wonderment. "Snippy little thing isn't he? Does he bite too?"

"If you get in the way, I shall bite your leg off," replied the feisty mouse.

Garth smiled and answered. "Well, I shall stay out of your way. This is becoming a day full of surprise and mystery."

Justin felt a cold wind at his back and decided that they had better push on. "It will be dark soon and we had better find open ground in case of attack again. I don't like being trapped on this road."

They gathered up the packs and put them on the now calm horse. Garth rode the mule with Pectin, which with his extra weight, slowed it even more. Garth finally jumped off the mule and said that he could walk faster.

After an hour of travel, the road came out of the ice canyon and into a small open clearing. There were still a few jagged crystals sticking up through the ground, but at least they had room to move in any direction, if need be. So they decided to stop and set up camp.

This far north the sun didn't set below the horizon as it did further south, so there was a small amount of light available to them. After all was readied for the night, Justin stood on a small mound of crystal ice and watched the horizon. Directly north, he could see a strange red glow above the hills and figured that it must have had something to do with Kyr. He shivered, not from the cold, but from the unknown forces ahead. He felt that Garth was right, that as long as they would all die if Kyr were free, then they may as well go down fighting.

Garth came up to Justin and stood beside him. "Well, boy, do you have a plan?"

"This may sound strange to you but the only way I can get to Kyr is by not knowing anything," He sighed. "I just have to take one danger at a time and hope to make the right decisions. With you here I feel we have a better chance now."

"Don't count heavily on me, boy. I'm a coward by nature, but I also don't like not knowing when I'm going to die. I will help you the best I can which, under the circumstances, may not be enough."

"Any help will be enough," comforted Justin to his companion. "Time to get some rest, morning will come early enough."

They went back to camp and crawled into their bed sacks. Sleep did not come easy for Justin that night.

CHAPTER SIX

MORNING did come early and Justin had only an hour of sleep, which didn't help his disposition. He was the first up and started to wake the others. Garth grumbled something that made Justin blush, and Pectin looked as though he couldn't believe that he were not at home in his bed.

The two mice stirred in the backpack as the men rolled their bed sacks and packed the camp. Nothing else was said as they did this, for everyone was feeling a strange uneasiness.

Justin mounted Canter and headed the horse northward followed by the night weary group. They stayed on the road as it twisted and turned until they reached a flat stretch of land surrounded by six huge crystals forming a circle around the road. This worried Justin as it looked like they had been arranged as such and to continue would mean going through the formation and being surrounded by it.

They slowly came into the center of the area when the ground started to rumble and shake. Justin jumped off Canter and tried to hold on to the reins to prevent the horse from bolting again. All around them the six tall crystal forms seemed to be reshaping, and as Justin watched, they formed into giant crystal men.

"Who are you and what are you doing here?" came a voice from above.

Justin looked up toward the origin of the voice and was surprised to find that it had a face.

"I am Justin of Freland and we are here at Mandara's bidding to complete a mission of good," bravely replied the frightened Justin. "Who do I have the pleasure of addressing?"

"You have no pleasure here and we have no name that you wish to speak. We are the guardians of the road to the Northland and if you wish to pass you will have to prove yourselves to us." The glass-like giant paused and then continued. "What is your mission? Speak the truth or perish as you stand," commanded the larger one, who seemed also to be the leader.

"We have been sent by Mandara to prevent Kyr from releasing himself from his imprisonment in the far Northland," answered Justin.

"What do you know of Kyr!" boomed the crystalline creature.

Justin bravely walked toward the monolith and spoke. "Kyr is the evil magical brother of Mandara the Magician and we have been sent here while the moon is red to prevent Kyr from freeing himself to destroy our world."

Crystal Prison of Kyr

"How do we know that you are not here to free Kyr?" demanded the glass giant.

"Since the moon became red, Kyr will be able to free himself without our help, so why should we bother to come here to free him since he will soon be able to do it on his own. We were sent here to stop him, as so many before us. Besides, if you are truly guardians, then you should be able to know the truth when it is spoken," bravely replied Justin.

"Answer our questions and we will know the truth when it is given, even if you are a very clever liar. If you have been sent here by Mandara, then you should be able to answer a simple question known only by the true savior," posed the crystal man.

"Ask and I shall answer truthfully."

"You will answer truthfully or be crushed where you stand," the monolith demanded. It paused, then continued carefully, "Tell me what form of prison holds Kyr."

Justin thought back on all that Mandara and Edan had said and had only one answer. "Ice," he spoke.

"Everything here is ice!!" the giant boomed. "I asked what FORM is his prison."

Justin felt a growing panic in his chest, as he could not remember anything about the shape of the ice that held Kyr. Quietly from Justin's pocket, Cheek whispered, "Justin, think back to Edan's last riddle, the one you said sounded like a statement. It will help you, think hard."

Justin strained to remember the riddle, but he had heard it only once and it was coming back in small bits. Something about glass, water and air. That could be ice, but not a shape. What was it about sides, a number? Five sides! Yes, he remembered five sides, but a box has six sides so it could not be a block of ice and definitely not a ball. He remembered something about four sides comparing, but what about the fifth? He looked up in desperation at the leader and saw the crystal point of its head. It had four sides and, of course, the base would be the fifth side. A pyramid! That had to be it!

Justin was about to speak but stopped. What if he was wrong? That would surely mean the death of his friends and he couldn't let that happen because of his blunder.

Crystal Prison of Kyr

"I shall answer your question, but I want to ask something of you first," He stood tall and continued. "If I am wrong, then do what you will with me, but please let my friends go back home to prepare for the destruction. I don't want them to die here in this land for my error."

The giant seemed to smile slightly and said, "You are brave and true to your companions, little man, but we make no deals. Answer the question and speak with your heart."

Justin summoned up his courage and spoke out loudly, "It's a pyramid!" He closed his eyes preparing to be crushed and as the ground rumbled again, he looked up to see the other five crystal men were reshaping back to their original harmless forms. The leader stood there for a moment before speaking.

"You may pass from here, brave one, and hurry for time grows short." He raised his crystal hand in a sign of salute and then reshaped back.

All was quiet after a moment and Justin turned to his white-faced companions.

Knowing they were frightened, he hoped to calm them by not showing any fear. "We better get going. Like he said, time grows short."

Justin mounted Canter and the party departed the gathering of the guardians. Cheek climbed up to Justin's shoulder and spoke into his ear. "Justin, I'm glad you paid attention to my little games with Edan. I'm proud of you, and I have no worries about the rest of the journey." He climbed back down into the pocket and Justin felt a growing pride inside.

They rode on for what seemed hours before anyone spoke, being still too shaken from the encounter with the guardians.

"Justin, I thought you weren't supposed to know anything about what was ahead and live to succeed," asked Pectin. "How did you know about the pyramid answer?"

"I didn't know, until the guardian asked his question, that a hand written riddle between Edan and Cheek had anything to do with Kyr. Edan knew about this journey, but couldn't say anything about it. Even though the last riddle between them was one of many simple riddles that Edan frequently shared with Cheek over the years, it also was the answer to the guardian's question. Since I didn't know that before this moment, I guess it didn't count as prior knowledge."

"The snake creature was a bad enough surprise, but to stand there in front of those ice men and not know if, and when, you'd die was worse," lamented Pectin.

"The fates are with us my friend. We will make it," smiled Justin.

"We'd better not run out of fates before we get there," warned Garth. "We'll need all the help we can get to deal with Kyr."

"The fates have put us together Garth, I have a feeling we will succeed," said Justin.

"I certainly hope so, because I think we will need the fates in a few minutes," Garth said as he stared ahead at the road.

Justin looked in that direction and saw what Garth was talking about. At the bottom of the hill, that they had just crossed over, was a bridge spanning across a wide gorge. Justin could see that it rose up over a very wide crack in the ground and that it was very long, shiny, narrow, and worst of all it looked to be made of slick ice. Justin started to worry since he had no idea as to how he was going to get everyone across it.

After they arrived at the bridge, the five of them stood looking down in to the abyss. It was too dark below to even see bottom. The chunk of ice that Garth had dropped made no sound hitting bottom, if there even was one.

Justin studied the bridge and knew that he wouldn't like to cross it. He also knew it would be even harder to get the animals to step out over the oblivion. It was about six feet wide with no sides and was made entirely of slippery looking ice. The other end was about twenty yards across, but it may as well been twenty miles.

"Garth, are you brave enough to cross this?" asked Justin.

"If I were drunk, maybe," wistfully remarked Garth.

"Well, we better do something soon or the sun will be gone for the night," reminded Cheek from his perch on Justin's shoulder. Kigamsti was comfortable looking out of

Justin's pocket and had no intentions on sitting up higher.

"I think we should camp here for the night and get a fresh start in the morning," said Justin, hoping to stall for time while he came up with an idea.

"Maybe so, Justin, but we'll have to make up for it later," replied Cheek, figuring Justin's real reasoning.

They set up camp and Justin wandered around looking for an answer to the problem, but all around him were ice crystals and chunks of broken trees, and nothing more. He stood looking at his horse and wondered how the beast could walk across the bridge without being frightened by the height or slipping on its hooves. He lifted one of the horse's legs and studied the horseshoe. It was soft metal and flat and not suited for ice. He was stumped for an answer, and decided to get some sleep. Maybe he could think better in the morning.

Everyone else was so worn out that they were already asleep. Justin got into his bed sack and lay there until fatigue overtook him.

Justin thought that he had just fallen asleep when he heard a faint voice calling him. He was surprised to see that it was morning. As the voice called again, he lifted his head, and saw Pectin on the other side of the bridge. Justin quickly jumped up and went to his side of the bridge calling to the still screaming and bouncing boy.

"Pectin, how did you get over there without sliding off?" he called.

"I crawled, stabbing my knives into the ice to hold me," he yelled back. "And it wasn't so bad since I couldn't see down, so I wasn't afraid."

Justin quickly thought about what Pectin had said about seeing down. That was the one thing that made them afraid to cross, the fear of falling down. If you couldn't see down, then you could do it. He thought that if he covered the animal's eyes, they would cross without fear. But would that keep them from slipping on their hooves? Garth came up next to Justin pulling on his coat.

"Now how did that fool boy get over there without killing himself?" he asked.

"Garth, I have part of an idea. If we cover the animal's eyes, they won't be afraid to cross. But I'm not sure how to keep them from slipping on the ice."

Garth thought for a minute and said, "Too bad we don't have some foot spikes like my hunter friends have to climb the ice hills."

Just then, an idea hit Justin. He ran to his sack and pulled out the file he used to sharpen his knife and rushed to the horse. Cheek and Kigamsti were now standing on the backpack wondering what he was up to. Justin lifted the hoof between his legs and started to file at it, making small crosshatched grooves in the hoof that left small sharp points in it. Garth was watching him and saw what he was doing.

"You got it!" he cried and ran to get his file. He started to work on the mule's hooves.

While they were busy at this, Pectin slid back across the bridge and then began breaking camp. Shortly the animals were loaded up and blindfolded and the mice were safely in Justin's pocket.

"Wait a minute," spoke Garth. "Someone has to lead the animals across the bridge or they'll blindly walk off the edge. What's to keep him from sliding off?"

Justin smiled. "We'll just have to be extra careful."

"We?" questioned Garth. "What do you mean WE?"

"You aren't afraid are you Garth?" Justin grinned, "Pectin got over and back by himself."

"He slid over on his belly with knives stuck into the ice, that's how he did it!"

"I was more afraid for the animals getting across than myself," scolded Justin. "I know that I can make it by foot."

"And what if the horse decides to get stubborn? Are you going to pull it across?" Garth demanded.

"I'll worry about that when it happens," answered Justin as he pulled Canter's reins. The horse resisted slightly so Justin talked to him nicely as he lead him to the bridge.

Pectin had already gone across and Justin told him to talk to the animals to let them know that someone friendly was ahead. Justin stepped out on to the bridge and slipped, nearly going over the side. If he hadn't been holding on tightly to Canter's reins, he would have been gone. Garth helped him up.

"Still want to walk across?" he said.

"I just have to get used to it. I wasn't ready," Justin replied nervously. He stepped out again and steadied himself. He kept saying repeatedly to himself, don't look down, don't look down!

Garth followed the horse pulling and politely cursing at the stubborn mule. He watched the horse's rear end so he wouldn't look down, and hoped that his leader didn't walk off the side as he would surely follow them down on a long death drop.

Pectin was shouting encouragement from the other side. Garth growled aloud that he wished the boy would shut up or that his shouts would cause an avalanche.

Garth wished he hadn't said that, for he heard a rumbling noise and had a strange feeling as to what it was. Looking back, he saw the snowcaps from the hills behind them sliding down toward the bridge.

"Justin! Run like hell, quick!" Garth screamed at the top of his lungs.

Justin looked back and saw the wall of snow heading toward them. They were about halfway across and this was no time to stop, so figuring the snow would push them off the bridge anyway, they took their chances on running.

Justin and Canter cleared the far side of the bridge and kept moving hoping that Garth was right behind him. He heard a scream and looked back expecting Garth and the mule to be gone, but Garth came around the rear of Canter, hollering.

"Couldn't you move any faster? I had my nose up the horse's butt trying to get past you!"

The rumbling and the wall of snow had ceased as it poured into the abyss and the two men stood there shaking. Garth looked at Justin and said, "We got to find a different way back. I'll be damned if I'll do that again!"

Both men let out a long well deserved laugh and hugged each other. It was then that Justin remembered the mice in his pocket and pushed back. He looked into the pocket and found it empty. His heart sank.

"Cheek!" he cried. "Cheek, where are you!"

"Don't worry Justin, we're all right."

He turned to the voice behind him and saw the two mice sitting on a rock. He ran to them and scooped Cheek up.

"How did you get here before me?" insisted Justin.

"When you first slipped, Kigamsti and I figured that we'd take our own chances and climbed off. Our claws helped us across."

Justin was relieved that they were safe and said so. He carefully let them crawl back into his pocket and turned to Garth and Pectin.

"Well, my brave crew, let's head on. We have more excitement to face."

CHAPTER SEVEN

THEIR SPIRITS were high as they rode on. They were feeling that nothing could stop them now as they ventured forth on the way to the enemy. It was probably all the excitement from the successful bridge crossing mixed with the happiness of being alive. Justin felt his blood rushing through his body and was feeling invincible.

Cheek could sense that Justin was being intoxicated by the excitement and decided it was time for a bit of restful diversion. He poked out from the pocket and looked up at his friend.

"Justin," he called up. "About two miles ahead is a side road to the left. Take the road and follow it to the end. We will stop there for a day."

Justin suddenly felt disappointed by the break in their journey and asked why. Cheek said that there was something that had to be done before they could go any further, and disappeared back into the pocket.

After a while, they came to the road and turned on to it. Garth complained about having to take the side trip. Justin told him what Cheek had said and that it was important, so the big man quieted down.

They had just come over a hill and saw something that they could not believe. Ahead, in a small valley of snow and ice, was a patch of green. In the middle of the forested area was a small town. Their spirits lifted again with the thoughts of getting out of the cold.

They crossed out of the snow into the grassy land and could feel warmth. Justin removed his cloak and felt the cold leave him. Pectin was asking if his place was enchanted and Justin replied that it probably was. Garth commented that he hoped the town had a tavern, and Justin thought to himself that he may even have a drink to celebrate getting this far.

Cheek popped out again and spoke to Justin. "When we enter the town, say nothing to anyone until I say so. There is one person who we must meet before we can do anything safely. Is that clear?"

"Yes, Cheek. Is there danger here?

"Not as long as you and the others do as I say. Tell them so." Justin relayed the orders to the others and they nodded in agreement.

They entered the town and quietly rode down through the center, being watched by the people now coming out to witness the ragged little parade. Justin saw that they looked like normal everyday folks, and wondered what they did here as he could see no businesses, and the stone buildings looked like simple homes. Children ran around them, jabbering excitedly but did not get in their way. Cheek and Kigamsti were watching from Justin's pocket as though they were expecting something. As they came to the far end of the town that stopped in front of a large dwelling, Cheek told Justin to stop and wait there.

After a moment, a large man came out of the building and approached them. He stopped before Justin and stood staring at him, which made Justin felt uneasy. He wished something would happen. Then it did.

Crystal Prison of Kyr

The door of the large building opened again and out walked a girl. She was wearing drab clothing and was rather plain looking. As she stood on the steps of the building, Justin noticed that she had a mouse on her shoulder. Justin looked from the mouse back to her face and suddenly recognized her as the girl in the mist. His mouth dropped and he almost said something when Cheek ran up to his shoulder and spoke in a loud voice.

"Althea, my mother, I have returned to you. I am Cheek, your son, taken by Edan the Elder to Freland many years ago."

The mouse on the girl's shoulder stood up and cried out. "Cheek, is it you, my son?"

Both mice found their way down to the ground and ran to each other. They hugged, danced, and cried. Justin was filled with emotion at the sight, knowing Cheek was reunited with his mother. Justin had lost his mother after his birth so he never knew what it was like to have a mother.

"Cheek, look at you, so grown up. I have missed you all these years." She looked up at Justin and asked, "Is this your master?"

"Yes mother, he is Justin and a good friend also. He is to be trusted."

"Well then, Cheek, it will be known by all that your master and his friends shall be trusted here."

With that, the man standing before Justin smiled and welcomed Justin and his friends. The townspeople came rushing toward them shouting their welcomes. Justin got down from Canter and came to Cheek and his mother. Bending down he asked Cheek to introduce him. Cheek did so, and when Justin looked up, he saw the girl standing before him. Justin stood and smiled.

"Hello, I'm Justin."

The girl smiled back and said, "Welcome Justin, I'm Kara, Althea's master and friend." She knelt down, picked up the two mice, and asked Justin to follow her. Justin turned to find that Garth and Pectin were busy talking to the crowd, so he followed her to the building.

The interior of the building was plain and simple. The furnishings were made of wood, and the walls were covered with tapestries.

Crystal Prison of Kyr

Justin was impressed by the plants, of which there were hundreds, scattered around the room.

"You have a very nice home here, Kara."

"Thank you Justin," she replied as she set the mice on the table. "I made it as comfortable as possible. Please sit down."

Justin sat at the table and watched Cheek conversing with his mother, while Kara brought out a bottle and into two mugs, she poured a clear liquid. She set one mug in front of Justin and raised hers to him.

"We shall toast to the return of Cheek, and to our new found friends," she said and drank.

Justin sipped the liquid and found it to be very tasty. It had a fruity flavor, and after he swallowed, he could taste a bit of wine in it. He drank more and felt a bit flushed for he was not much of a drinker.

"Careful with that wine, Justin, it goes down smooth but kicks like a mule," Cheek warned the boy.

"I think it's delicious," and to Kara, "Do you make this?"

"Everything we eat and drink is made here. We have learned to grow much in such a small area. The constant weather is perfect for growing year round."

"I didn't see any cattle. Where do you get your meat?"

"We're vegetarians, so we have no livestock. It also saves on having to feed them," she smiled.

Justin stared at her smile for it had been on his mind and in his dreams for the past week. She noticed his stare and asked, "Is there something wrong with my face?"

"Oh, no, I... I was just thinking about something. I was sure that I've seen you before, somewhere," squirmed Justin.

"Not unless you've been here before. I have never left the valley," she smiled again. "And I'm sure that I would have remembered you."

Justin was becoming intoxicated by both the wine and her smile. He set the wine down and concentrated on her smile. Kara went into another room, saying that she would prepare a meal for them. Althea said something to Cheek and she scurried down the table to follow Kara.

Justin suddenly remembered Kigamsti was still in his pocket and looked in to see what the black mouse was doing. Justin was surprised to find his pocket was empty.

"Cheek, do you know where Kigamsti went?"

Cheek ran over to Justin and spoke quietly. "Justin, please don't mention anything about him yet. A mouse without a master is not welcome here. Later you must explain to Pectin that he is to say that he is Kigamsti's master."

Justin nodded and told Cheek that he would go tell him now before they say anything to the townspeople. He called to Kara to say that he was going to check on his friends, and would be back shortly.

Justin left the house to find that his friends were not to be seen. He asked a man walking by if, he knew where they were and the man pointed out a building across the way and said they were in there. Justin thanked him and went to the building. It was a small tavern, which probably pleased Garth. Justin's eyes adjusted to the dim light and saw his friends seated in the middle of the room. Garth was busy telling his tale of conquering the snake beast and Pectin was looking bored. Justin called to Pectin, and when the boy came over, he told him what Cheek had said. Pectin said that he would do Cheek's bidding and told Justin that Kigamsti was in his pocket already. Justin was relieved to know that the mouse was safe and went back to Kara's home.

After the sumptuous meal, Justin helped clear the table and the conversation was mostly about the town and the people there. After a while, they went out to the porch and sat on a bench facing north. The sun was low behind the mountains and the eerie red glow was starting to be visible in the northern sky.

"I have heard tales of Kyr and what would happen if he were loose," Kara said to Justin, "Do you think that you will be able to stop him?"

"I hope so," Justin answered. "I still don't know what to do when I get there. I'll just have to worry about it when it happens."

Crystal Prison of Kyr

Cheek looked up to Justin and said, "Justin, it's time that I tell you why we stopped here. We came to pick up someone to go with us. That someone is Kara."

Justin and Kara both looked surprised and Justin said, "Cheek, the journey is too dangerous to take her. I won't allow it."

"I'm sorry Justin, but it has to be so or we will surely fail."

"But why Kara? Aren't there any strong, brave men here who could go?"

"It has nothing to do with being strong or brave or men. Kara is the only one we must take and I can't say any more. It has to be." Then Cheek crawled up on Kara's lap and continued, "Kara, you must go willingly, but it is extremely important that you do. Are you brave enough to help save our world?"

Kara thought a moment and answered. "Cheek, I could sit here till doom comes and die a coward, but I will go with you to help. What is it I must do?"

"Pack warmly and ask no more questions. That is all I can say for now. I will explain more when we reach Kyr."

Cheek climbed down and he and his mother went back into the building. Justin sat there thinking, afraid of anything happening to Kara, but also a little glad that she would be with him longer.

"Kara, I swear on my life that no harm shall come to you. I will be your protector on the journey."

"Thank you Justin, I hope I will sleep better knowing that." She smiled again.

"I hate not knowing anything and the mystery of why you must go there," Justin said as he stood. He went down the steps followed by Kara. They walked in silence toward a flower garden on the side of the house. They stood there watching the red fire light in the sky, not speaking. Kara moved close to Justin and he put his arm around her. They looked into each other's eyes for a long moment then felt a little embarrassed by this.

"I feel as though I have known you for years," spoke Justin finally. "I first saw you in a mist at Mandara's cavern. He knew we were going to meet and I'm glad for it. I have thought of little else but you for the past week. It was the one thing that helped get me through the journey so far, and now I am actually with you."

"I'm also glad you're here," she spoke softly. "I have had a dream that someday a handsome young man would come to rescue me from the valley. I love it here, but I am lonely for companionship. The young men in town all treat me as though they were forbidden to be with me. My life so far has been as mysterious as your journey. With you here I feel as though my life is going to change for the better despite having to go to Kyr."

"We will get through this together, and after it all, I'll be there to protect you." Justin spoke as though he felt an emptiness were being filled inside. "I feel the fates have brought us together."

They looked again deep into each other's eyes and gently kissed. From behind them, a small deep voice cleared its throat and said, "I think it's time for you two to get some sleep, for we still have a long journey to go."

They turned to see Cheek standing on the porch. They smiled to each other and with Cheek, went into the house. Later, as Justin lay on the soft quilt bed, his head was filled with daydreams of Kara. Her smile was the last thing he saw as he fell asleep.

CHAPTER EIGHT

JUSTIN AWOKE feeling more rested than he had since the beginning of the trip, probably due to the feather bed and the warmth of the room. All was quiet as he walked into the main room and wondered where everyone else was.

He opened the front door and looked out to find Pectin getting the horses ready. Garth was sitting on the steps looking like he had indulged a little too much of the valley wine. He was holding his head and groaning. Justin stepped up behind him and said good morning loudly in his ear. The big man howled and jumped from the porch.

"Don't ever do that again when I'm thinking," he growled.

"You mean don't do that after you've been drinking," laughed Justin. "Head a little big this morning?"

"About two sizes too big. What is that stuff they make?" he moaned.

"I don't know, but I stopped after one mug." He looked to Pectin and asked, "Has Cheek informed you of our new traveling companion?"

"Yes, he told me earlier this morning. He woke me rather rudely too," grimaced Pectin. "I'm not as bad feeling as Garth, but I would rather not have been woken before sunrise."

Around the side of the building came Mr. Symms, the man they first encountered when they entered the town. He was bringing a horse for Kara. Justin had found out from Cheek that he was Kara's guardian and spoke very little, which is why he seemed a little mysterious and didn't look like he fit in with the rest of the townspeople. Justin figured that Cheek would further explain everything later and it all would still be clear as mud.

Justin heard a door open and turned to the building to see Kara coming out. He ran up the steps to her and took the large pack that she was carrying.

"Good Morning, Kara, I hope you slept as well as I did."

"I slept well for about an hour, but I think I will survive." She gave him that smile again and Justin's heart melted. He hoped that he could keep his mind on the task ahead and not on her so much. He knew it wouldn't be easy.

"Where is Althea?" Justin inquired.

"She is staying here with Mr. Symms. Cheek insisted that she was not needed on the journey." Her smile dropped a little. "I'm glad for that but I'll miss her."

"I know how you feel. I'm lost without Cheek when he's not around."

"Do you know how long it will take to reach Kyr?" She asked.

"Cheek said last night that it will be about a four day ride from here. If all goes well and

we aren't stopped by one of Mandara's traps."
He frowned, thinking about taking her on such
a dangerous mission.

"Don't worry Justin, I'll be alright." She put
her hand on his cheek and the warmth made
him feel good. It was almost as if she could
read his mind, and not really knowing
anything about her, he thought it would be
better to be careful what he was thinking, just
in case.

"I don't like taking a woman on this trip,"
growled Garth from behind.

"I'm Sorry Garth, but Cheek said it is to be
so, and he seems to know more than he will
admit. For good reasons I hope."

"Well, I want it known that I disapprove,"
grumbled the big man.

"So noted, my friend. Now I think I had
better find Cheek and get this group on its
way." Justin went to the house and found
Cheek saying good-bye to his mother. Cheek
turned to Justin and jumped onto his friend's
outstretched hand. Cheek took one last look at
his mother and said to Justin that they should
go. Justin went back outside and found

everyone was mounted and ready to go. He noticed that the mule had been replaced by a fresh horse. Garth now also had his own stead, which would make things easier on the journey.

"Justin, ask Pectin if he has Kigamsti with him?" Cheek sounded a little worried. Justin inquired of Pectin as to the whereabouts of "his" mouse and Pectin replied that the creature was safe with him.

They headed out of the village as the townspeople watched quietly. Justin thought this was odd as they should have been cheering them on, but they probably were more concerned for Kara's safety. They left the green valley and made it back to the main road. Garth was grumbling about the cold and Pectin kept telling him to shut up, causing the big man would shoot back with an insult to the boy. At least they were funny enough to keep everyone's mind off the journey ahead.

They traveled mostly in silence as the days wore on and they stopped to rest as little as they could to save time. The sun was getting lower in the sky, but would never go below the horizon this far north. Even though it would never get totally dark, they would eventually have to stop to sleep. It wasn't long before Cheek suggested to Justin that they should find a spot to rest. Justin found a small area that looked good for a camp and told the others to set up there.

They were all quite tired from the trip and the short rest that they had in the town had made them a bit too lazy to be energetic. Everyone but Justin and Kara had climbed into their bed sacks and drifted off into sleep. The young couple sat on a blanket before the fire and just stared into it.

"I wonder what is ahead for me," Kara broke the silence.

"It must be important or Cheek would have never taken you along," replied Justin. "You must have a great deal to do with preventing Kyr from being free. I guess that my task is to see that you get there safely."

Kara looked lost in her thoughts, years away from where they sat before the fire. "I feel sad, and yet relieved, that I am finally away from the valley and maybe finding out what my life is all about. I have been raised and pampered there without knowing why. Mr. Symms has seen to my education and protection, and I never knew my parents, since no one seems to know what happened to them. They just disappeared when I was small. My life has been one big mystery and maybe this is a way to find out something." She paused to reflect on her life and Justin had no words to comfort her. He thought of how he had never known his mother and barely had any time with his father before he was killed in the war.

"I'm sure that all will come together and soon you will be free to get on with your life," Justin said as he thought of how he'd like to be part of that life. Her face and hair looked so beautiful before the fire and he wanted so much to kiss her again as he had the night before.

She looked to him with a smile again. Justin panicked, had she read his mind about the kiss? She looked deep into his eyes, then leaned toward him, and gently kissed him. Justin felt warm and yet embarrassed by the kiss. He wanted so much to hold her but kept his thoughts hidden, just in case.

"I think we should get some sleep, we should try to be rested for tomorrow," offered Justin, changing the subject before his thoughts gave him away. "I will be close by in case of danger, so don't worry."

She smiled again and said, "With you near me, I will sleep well. Thank you Justin." She gently kissed him again and went to her bed sack. Justin waited a few moments till she was safely tucked in. He then went to his bed sack and laid there for what seemed hours before he fell asleep.

It was a long quiet night for the small party of heroes who were now all sleeping soundly, not hearing the strange movements around them in the semi-dark. They would not know of the terror of what was happening until they awoke that morning.

Justin heard Cheek mumbling something. His mind was still groggy, but he was certain that Cheek was tugging at his ear, and saying something about being in trouble. He sat up quickly, dropping Cheek off onto the ground. He blinked his weary eyes and looked to the small mouse, still yelling at him.

"Justin! Wake up! We have a problem here!" The tiny creature was frenzied.

"What is it Cheek? What problem?" He yawned. His eyes focused ahead and the hair on his neck stood up at what he saw. He jumped up and stood looking around the camp. Sometime during the early morning, someone or something had put a huge ice cage around them. Justin ran to the crystal clear bars that imprisoned them. They were about one arm's length around and so close together that he could just barely get his hand through.

"Garth! Pectin! Get up! We have a problem!" He cried.

"That's what I said!" yelled Cheek.

"What's the matter now?" grumbled Garth as he woke and his eyes went wide as he saw the cage. "Fates preserve us, what happened?"

"I don't know. I heard nothing during the night. It's as though it were poured over us and frozen." Justin rounded the perimeter trying to find an opening.

Garth and Pectin were now pushing and pulling at the bars with no luck. Kara sat up in her bed sack, but Justin asked her not to move. He stood at the center of the huge structure and surveyed the sides and top. It did look as though it were poured from a point at the top, too high to climb and far too slippery.

"Now what do we do?" cried Pectin as he tried to hack away at the crystal bar with his knife. It was frozen so hard that the blade made barely a dent in it.

They all felt an icy shiver run through them as they heard an inhuman growl from around the closest hill. They watched as a huge, hairy beast, walking upright like a man, came around the side of the hill. It came toward them and up to the cage as everyone ran to the far side of the area away from the creature. It was tall enough to look down at them from the top of the cage. Justin remembered his sword and ran to his pack. As he fumbled for it, he heard screams from his friends, and as he looked up he saw a hairy hand above him. Grabbing his sword, he slashed at it with all his strength. The beast made a howling cry at the small wound in its finger and pulled back.

"Oh good, make him mad!" yelled Garth.

"What would you have me do, let him pick me up to say hello?" screamed Justin.

The beast stomped on the ground with his foot causing the small people to lose their footing. The creature stomped away back around the hill and was gone, for the moment. It grew quiet after a while as the party listened for a sound of its whereabouts.

"We have to get out of here," demanded Pectin.

"Do you have a suggestion boy?" barked the big man.

"Quiet down, both of you, and think." Justin ordered the two as he paced the cage walls. "The bars are made of ice! If we could build a fire around one, then we could get out."

Pectin ran to the firewood but stopped in panic. "Justin! The creature has frozen the wood in ice. We'll never get it out."

Justin had to think fast. He needed heat to melt the bars, and without the wood there could be no fire. He stood there looking at his breath and thinking about how cold it was. He didn't shiver, despite the cold, and thought of how he was warm in the magic cloak that Mandara had given him. His mind started to wander when it hit him. "My cloak! It gives off a heat of its own depending on how cold the wearer is! If I can get it around one of the bars, maybe it will melt it enough to get out."

"We need a roaring fire to melt these bars, not a cape!" roared Garth.

"It can't hurt to try," said Justin as he tried to reach around one smaller bar with the cloak, but couldn't get his arm through. "Great, I can't reach."

Cheek and Kigamsti came running over to him, "Justin, give us one corner of the cloak and we will pull it around to the other side."

Justin pushed the cloak through the bar, and the mice ran out pulling the cloth around the bar to the other side, enough for Justin to pull it back through. He slid the cape up around the block of ice and held it together at the opening. It started to feel warmer in his hands and after a few moments, it started to get hot. He fastened the clasp and let go. Water started dripping down the sides of the ice bar and everyone let out a cry of joy at the sight. The water was coming faster now and Justin told everyone to pack quickly.

"Where are the horses?" cried Pectin.

In the panic, no one had noticed that they were gone. "Great, the creature ate them," moaned Garth.

"Let's just get out of here, and then we'll worry about the horses," ordered Justin. The bar was getting smaller now and everyone carried as much as they could of the supplies.

Justin watched as the bar melted faster and watched for the beast, hoping to be out before its return. Every so often, he had to adjust the cape tighter so it wouldn't slip down. It was very hot and Justin's hands were hurting from the adjustments. The bar finally was small enough that Justin ran against it with his shoulder and it gave way with a crack. Everyone cheered and started scrambling to get out. Justin gathered up the cloak and found it had cooled quickly to where he could put it on. He led his friends away from the cage toward the hill.

"Unfortunately we have to go down the trail past the point where the beast went. We'll have to take our chances that it won't see us." Justin said quietly to the frightened group.

Crystal Prison of Kyr

They made their way to the hill where they last saw the creature. As they came around the corner, they stopped. There was a sort of ice dwelling that must have been the creature's home. In front of the house was a large pot over a fire. Justin figured the beast was melting ice for the water it used to make the cage, or worse, to cook them in. Just to the left of the building were the horses in an ice corral. Justin wondered how he got the horses there without them making noise.

"We've got to get them or we'll never make it to Kyr in time," whispered Justin. The beast was nowhere to be seen. They stood there a few minutes, thinking, when they heard a noise from behind them. Turning, they saw the creature had come around the other side of the hill to the cage, and finding it empty, became angry. It was heading their way but had not spotted them yet.

"Run to the house! Quickly!" he said and was on his way. He led the group around the back of the building before the beast could see them. It came to the building and walked to the corral to check the horses. Satisfied that they were still there, it stood there puzzled by the disappearance of the humans. Justin was trying to figure out how to subdue the beast so they could rescue the horses and get away. He came around the opposite side of the building from the creature and studied the water pot. It was hanging from a bar supported by posts. Justin thought that if the posts were knocked over, the pot would spill, and if they could get the creature to walk into the water, maybe it would be stuck as the water froze. It was a risk but the only one Justin could think of. He came back and told the others of his plan. They came back around the building and saw the creature just standing where it had been. The men ran to the side of the pot unseen by the beast.

They studied the post, and found that if they could pull one of the supports outward, the thing would be unbalanced and fall. They frantically worked the support out as they kept an eye on the creature. It was just standing there in some sort of thought. The post started to sway as the support gave way then they pushed, hoping to make the pot fall toward the creature, and it did. The water poured down toward the beast in a wave. It splashed the legs and feet of the beast and settled around him. Justin hoped the ground was cold enough to freeze the water quickly. As the hairy creature howled in surprise and turned to see what was happening, it slipped on the watery ice and came down on its side. It tried to get up but slipped again. The water was beginning to crystallize, the beast's hair was sticking to the ground, and finally it was trapped in the ice and could not move. It laid there howling at the top of its lungs.

The men cheered and hollered in delight that the plan had worked. Justin yelled to them to get everything together and get the horses packed. They worked frantically to get away, although the beast could not move. Kara stood safely from the beast and said to Justin, "I feel sorry for him. He will die laying there."

Cheek poked his head out from Justin's pocket and replied, "Don't worry about him. As soon as the afternoon sun gets overhead, he will warm up enough to get free, and we will be long gone from here."

Justin was impressed by Kara's compassion for the beast that almost killed all of them. She had a good heart and that made him care about her even more. The horses were packed and everyone mounted up to leave the beast. It lay there watching them go and let out a blood-curdling howl. Justin looked back and wondered if they would have to deal with the beast on the way back.

"Cheek," inquired Justin "Will we have to go back through all these dangers to get out of the Northlands?"

"Don't worry about getting out until we see if we can get in. Then we'll worry about getting back," sighed the mouse perched on Justin's shoulder.

They rode on again in silence, other than Garth's occasional comments complaining about the cold, or having a woman on the journey. Pectin would quiet him by reminding him that he could always go back, making the big man just scowl even more. They made camp that evening and Justin made a schedule for the men to take turns watching the camp. Garth growled some more.

The next few days were traveled without any problems. Cheek and Kigamsti seemed to spend more time together chattering away. Justin figured that they were plotting something for when they arrived at Kyr's pyramid. At night, the reddish glow from Kyr grew in intensity, bringing a chill to Justin's spine. He wasn't really afraid, just worried. What if he failed? What if one of them was killed along the way? What if something happened to Kara? He stopped thinking about it before he went crazy with worry.

Cheek finally announced that they would be to Kyr's land the next day. Everyone was silent at the announcement, not knowing whether to be happy that it was almost over, or worried about what was to come. The last few days had been uneventful and that worried Justin even more. It had been too quiet. Was the worst to come before they would get to Kyr?

They set up camp that evening and everyone sat quietly around the fire thinking about the next day. Justin sat with his arm around Kara, basking in the warmth of her and the fire. Cheek and Kigamsti were still off chattering their secrets, or maybe just having a good time telling mouse tales. Garth finally broke the silence.

"I just want to say that I am sorry if I complained a bit too much. It's just my way of blowing off steam. Justin, you have done well to get us this far and I know all will go well tomorrow."

"We'll make it safely back to our homes and Kyr will be put in his place for a while again," offered Pectin.

Justin just smiled and thanked his friends for coming. He felt that he could have made the journey alone but Garth and Pectin made it more enjoyable despite their bickering.

They all said their good nights and went off to sleep. Justin lay there watching Kara's bed sack and wondering what was in store for her tomorrow. He drifted off just about the time that Pectin awoke him to take his turn at watch. Justin sat sleepily in the silence wondering if he would ever get a good night's rest again, or after tomorrow would he die and spend eternity sleeping.

CHAPTER NINE

THE WIND was howling more and more as Justin sat there watching the camp. He was weighing all the options that lay before him as to whether he would be able to finish the task thrust upon him or not. He had made a free choice as to whether he would go or not, but the way everyone had pushed and honored him, he wondered if he really had a free choice in going. What if he had refused? Would they have chosen another to go in his place? There wasn't really enough time to choose someone else to complete the task, so would they have accepted his refusal so easily or talked him back into it?

His mind raced with more and more dumb thoughts as the hour to meet Kyr arrived. It helped him forget the danger ahead and helped keep his mind sharp for tomorrow. He wanted to sleep so badly that he became worried he would make the wrong decision tomorrow and end the world as he knew it. Life was not so easy, he determined, and since it was so quiet lately, he decided to get a few moments sleep. He sat back against the rock he was perched on and closed his eyes. The next thing he knew was that he was being slapped on the face repeatedly, by Garth, trying to wake him.

"Justin, wake up! Kara's gone!" he kept repeating. What he was saying finally sunk into Justin's head and he jumped up in panic.

"What! Where is she?" He questioned.

"How the blazes should I know!" Garth replied. "I got up and she is nowhere to be seen."

Justin's chest tightened, and he was upset at the thought that he had fallen asleep on guard duty and let her be taken. He ran around searching for her, but she was nowhere to be seen. Cheek poked his head out of the back sack that he and Kigamsti slept in and demanded to know what was going on. Garth told him and Cheek went into a total frenzy.

"We are doomed if she is gone! Find her now or all is lost," the tiny mouse screamed at the top of his tiny lungs.

Finally, everyone was up and searching the area for the missing girl. She was gone. Justin was in a daze that he had let this happen. Garth was yelling to the others to look here and there around the area.

Further searching, they could not produce the missing girl. Justin checked the ground for footprints and found none. It was as though she had been spirited away or flown off by winged creatures in the night. Justin had a vision of doom for his world and felt responsible. Justin took a rest and sat, as Garth sat next to him and put his arm around the boy.

"Justin, don't worry, we'll find her. I understand the strain that you have been through. It will work out, don't worry."

Justin could not be comforted by his friend's words. He had gotten everyone this far only to fail. Cheek ran up his shoulder and pulled on his ear.

"Justin, stop feeling like you failed! We got this far and we will succeed! You have to pull yourself together and get us the rest of the way. Besides, Kara needs you now more than ever." Justin felt as though his tiny friend could read his mind and felt a bit better. He had to get on with what had to be done. She was not gone, just missing for now, and he would find her or die.

Justin stood up and announced, "If she is anywhere, then it has to do with Kyr. We will go there, find her, and stop him!" He packed his things quickly and was mounted on Canter before the rest had finished. He took off down the road despite Cheek's warnings to wait for the rest of the group, but Justin was hot and moving. He raced on, being told where to go by the reluctant Cheek, hoping that Kigamsti would guide the rest of the party to their destination.

Justin traveled on for what seemed hours and Cheek clutched on for dear life. Justin was now a man determined to find the woman he loved, and to stop the one thing that threatened his happiness. After a while, they came to a wall of ice in the road and Justin halted Canter as he studied the structure. It reminded him of Mandara's wall of stone and how the opening had been so cleverly concealed. He didn't know how Pectin had opened Mandara's door and cursed himself for not asking. He thought to himself about how he would get into Mandara's world, if he only knew the secret. He remembered how Pectin had stared at the wall and concentrated on the opening. He stared hard and thought of the wall sliding up to reveal the entrance. Nothing happened.

He thought of how he so badly wanted to get into the world beyond, and concentrated on that. He envisioned being inside and concentrated hard on it. After a moment, there was a slight rumbling as the wall slid up to reveal a large opening in the ice. He kicked the reluctant horse on and they entered the opening. There was a strange glow all around them as they traveled down a path that twisted and turned much like Mandara's cavern. After what seemed hours, they came out into an opening of brilliant red light. Ahead Justin could see the huge pyramid that imprisoned the evil magician.

Canter stopped on his own and reared up, dropping Justin and Cheek to the ground. The frightened horse turned back up the trail that they had just came down and bolted. Justin screamed for the horse but it was gone. Cheek lay on the trail without moving and Justin panicked at the sight of his lifeless friend.

"Cheek! Get up! Don't die on me!" he screamed at the top of his lungs. "I don't know what to do!"

The mouse still laid there without moving. Justin scooped his friend up and put him in his pocket. He stood up and faced the pyramid, tears streaming down his cheeks and screamed at the monolith, "I hate you Kyr! You are destroying everything I love! I will stop you no matter how powerful you are! And don't think that I can't!"

He ran on foot toward the structure, and upon reaching it he tried to climb up, but slid back down the side. He tried again, and again slid down the crystal walls. He stood there in frustration, then ran around the side to see if there was a better way up. As he came around the back of the pyramid, he stopped in shock as he saw a small block of ice with a familiar form imprisoned in it. It was Kara.

He ran to the block and beat on it with his fists. He kept beating and beating until his hands were bloodied. He stopped when he heard a loud crying noise behind him. He turned, expecting to see some monster, but was shocked to see himself kneeling and sobbing in the snow. The figure was in pain and begging Justin to stop, but he was beginning to realize that nothing here could be real. He turned to the ice block holding his beloved Kara only to find it contained a skeleton. He screamed and turned back towards the ghost of himself. He ran to it and grabbed it by the throat pulling it up to him.

"Tell me where she is or I will strangle the Fates out of you!!" he roared. His image just smiled and then turned into frightened Pectin. Justin let the vision go, not knowing who he was hurting. The form before him reared up, and this time it was Garth, holding a large sword above its head ready to bring it down on the boy. Justin fell to the ground at the sight of his friend ready to kill him and held his arms up in defense. The figure stood there for a moment ready to strike and stopped. It had a sickly smile on its face, and then screamed in pain as the image of Garth faded into a slimy mask of death.

The creature suddenly sprouted wings and tried to fly up, but something was attached to its back. Justin watched in horror as the ugly creature turned around and there was the real Garth, hanging from the knife blade he had stabbed the creature with. The two of them rose up into the air and seemed to falter as the knife met home somewhere in the creature's body. They both crashed to the ground and Garth struggled to get away from the writhing mass of melted flesh that screamed and shook on the ground. After a moment, the creature was silent and unmoving. Garth sat in shock at what he had done, as Justin ran over him.

"Garth, are you all right?" cried Justin.

"I will be as soon as we get out of here, you stupid boy!" Garth retorted.

"When did you get here?"

"In time to save your butt!" replied the visibly shaken man. "Did you find the girl?"

Justin turned to the block of ice and there was Kara, still imprisoned there. He pulled Garth's head toward the block and pointed.

"Glad to see she's still with us," he grimaced.

Pectin came around the opposite corner of the pyramid as Justin helped Garth up. "Oh, am I so glad to see you two!" he cried. "I got lost around the other side of this thing."

Garth spoke quickly, "We followed behind you as fast as we could without being able to understand that stupid mouse Kigamsti. He just kept climbing all over me chattering away. I stuffed him in my pocket to shut him up, and if it weren't for the hoof prints in the snow, we wouldn't have known where you went."

"Thank you for being here my friend. I'd be dead if you hadn't gotten here in time," offered Justin to the big man.

Crystal Prison of Kyr

"Don't thank me yet, until you deal with that," he said looking toward the large pyramid.

They all stared at the glowing form as the thing started to flicker in color from red to orange reminding Justin of the first night he saw the moon shimmer. Justin jumped up and ran to the block of ice holding Kara intact. He removed his cloak and threw it over the form hoping it would help. The ground started to shake, knocking the men off their feet.

The top of the pyramid started to glow a white-hot color and seemed to melt away. Justin watched both the pyramid and Kara's ice prison as they both were racing to melt. He heard a booming voice in his head calling to him; it was saying that the time was over for him and his friends.

Justin jumped up and ran around the pyramid hoping to distract Kyr away from his friends and his beloved Kara. Since it was Justin who was supposed to stop Kyr, he hoped that Kyr would worry about him first.

The top of the pyramid seemed to dissolve into brilliant light and energy that blew off into space leaving only half a pyramid. At the top of the remaining structure stood the form of a man. He stretched as though he had not moved in a long time. Justin knew it was Kyr, freed from his bonds.

Kyr laughed at the top of his lungs, an evil laugh that made the hair on Justin's body rise. Justin stood tall and yelled bravely up to Kyr, "Don't think you are free yet evil one!"

Kyr looked slowly down at the boy and raised his hand up. As he brought his hand down a bolt of red light streamed forth toward Justin but missed him. Justin wasn't sure if he missed him on purpose or that he was a bit rusty being imprisoned for so long. He hoped for the rust and ran around the side of the building. Kyr tried again to blast him and again missed. He seemed annoyed that his aim was off and flew down to Justin's level. He landed hard and made the ground shake. The evil one was definitely off in his timing, much to Justin's delight. If he could stall him long enough for Kara to be released, then there may be hope. But without Cheek to help, Justin didn't know what Kara could do. Justin kept running around the pyramid until he realized that he was back where Kara was. He couldn't turn back for Kyr was right behind him. The block of ice was not melting as fast as he would have liked and Garth and Pectin were nowhere to be seen.

Justin turned to see Kyr fly around the pyramid. As he got closer, he kicked the boy in the head, then landed, unsteadily, just beyond where he fell. Justin lay on the ground nearly knocked silly and raised his weary head to see Kyr standing before him smiling wickedly.

Justin was helpless on the ground, not able to move a muscle as the dark figure came over him. The sinister being paused a moment, raised its arms toward the boy, and then as the demon's face glowed, radiant energy shot from its hands. Justin could feel his body being enveloped in the painful rays and could feel his soul going numb. As his brain fought the torturous pain, his thoughts relived the events of the last week that brought him to this agony. In a small part of his mind, he could see himself sitting safely in his home, reviewing his schoolbooks, and for a brief moment, relived it.

As Justin's mind returned to the present, he saw Kyr raise his hand and blast Kara's ice block with a red beam of light that blew off the cape and made the ice glow. The glow seemed to turn from red to blue and suddenly shot back at Kyr. He was knocked off his feet, but he quickly got up, with a panicked look on his face. The ice block glowed brighter in a blue light and this seemed to frighten the evil one. Kyr turned his powers on the ice wall above the block, and started to melt it, causing water to pour on Kara's block, freezing her deeper in ice. Justin wanted to strangle the magician, but he couldn't move.

While Kyr held his attentions on melting the ice, he didn't notice Garth and Pectin sneaking up behind him. They pounced on him, but they were both flung off by Kyr's increasing strength. He turned to them, and spotted Pectin first, he pointed toward the boy. A burst of red light streamed out from his hand and enveloped the youth. As Pectin screamed in pain, he managed to throw his knife at the magician. It flew toward Kyr who caught it in his hand and flung it back at the boy. It rammed deep into the boy's chest and he slumped to the ground, lifeless.

Garth, lying flat on his back, felt a stirring in his pocket. Kigamsti ran out to witness Pectin's demise. The tiny mouse ran up to a nearby rock and stood up as tall as he could. Out of him came a human-like scream that shook the walls around them. Kyr was visibly shaken by the scream, as though he recognized the sound. Kigamsti stood there staring into Kyr's eyes and Kyr could not move. Justin could not believe what he was seeing, for Kigamsti was changing his form. He grew into a large dark figure against the light and Justin was stunned to realize that it was Mandara!

Kyr was also stunned. The two brothers stood there looking at each other as Mandara spoke in a booming voice. "Kyr, my brother! You are evil and I hate and deny you! I give myself unto the evil side of Fates by destroying you!" Mandara screamed and flew up into the air toward the shocked Kyr before he could react. Mandara landed on Kyr with his hands around his brother's throat, strangling the life out of him. They both were enveloped in a yellow light that grew so bright that Justin could not look at it any longer. He turned away until it faded. After a moment he looked back to find Mandara standing over the lifeless form of his brother.

Mandara ran to the body of Pectin and lifted the boy up from the ground. He carried him to Kara's ice block and set him before her. He removed his cloak and placed it around the ice imprisoning the girl. The ice started to quickly melt. Justin tried to get up, but he was still hurt and dazed. With Garth's help, they went to where the others were.

Mandara pulled the cloak off the now thawed form of Kara and she blinked in wonder as to where she was. Mandara held his hand up to her and helped her down from the last of the ice.

"Kara you must pull the blade from his body to save him," spoke Mandara, pointing to Pectin. "I don't have the power to do so. Killing my brother has left me virtually powerless. Please help him, you have the power."

She looked puzzled, but went to Pectin and pulled the knife out of his chest. From all around Pectin and Kara came a soft glow of light. As the light faded, he groaned and let out a sigh. After a moment, he blinked and looked around at his friends. He smiled and said, "Did I get him?"

They all laughed and Mandara, holding Pectin, said to him, "Yes my son, you did."

CHAPTER TEN

"WHAT do you mean I missed it!!" moaned Cheek as he was coming out of his unconscious state. He was dazed but all right, which made everyone happy. "I can't believe that I came all this way, plotting and worrying, only to have missed the best part of it all!"

"Sorry Cheek, but when Canter threw us, you were knocked out," laughed Justin at his friend's misfortune. "I'm just glad that you are all right."

"I can't believe it!" the mouse moaned.

"Don't worry my little friend, I'll have Fog show you everything that happened," comforted Mandara. "Safely in my cavern."

"It won't be the same," grumbled Cheek.

The group was gathered around the tiny mouse laying on a rock. Justin went to Mandara wanting to know answers to many questions.

"Justin, my young savior, I thank you from the bottom of my ancient heart for delivering me here safely to my brother. You will go down in history for this." The magician hugged the boy, then let him loose turning back to Cheek. "Master Cheek, I'm sorry you missed the battle, but I also want to thank you for helping me. Your mother will be proud of you."

"Mandara, why didn't you tell me that you were coming along, and why as a mouse?" inquired Justin.

"Justin, if you had known that I was with you, we would have never have gotten this far. It was the element of surprise that I needed. Since Kyr would have focused his attention on the leader of the group, he would have sensed in your mind that I was here and with what powers he had available, would have destroyed me before I could get to him. As for my form as a mouse, I could never have gotten here as a human. It was part of my safeguard spell so that I would never weaken and decide to let my brother loose. The spell prevented any human with knowledge of this land from coming here to get to Kyr. I would have been destroyed as a human when I entered this cavern by the energy in the pyramid. So I figured that if I weren't human, that I might get here safely as a mouse."

"Might get here? You weren't sure?" asked Garth.

"I didn't really know how well I had cast the spell. I never said that animals couldn't enter the land, so I tried it as Kigamsti the mouse. It worked."

"If you had all the intentions of coming here and destroying your brother, what was my purpose in being here?" wondered Justin thinking that he was now nothing more than a delivery boy.

"Justin, don't belittle your importance on the quest. Even though I was with you, I could do absolutely nothing to help or else give myself away. I put all my faith in you to get us here safely, and you didn't disappoint me. Edan chose well when he recommended you and I'm glad for it. You are a hero and have battled Kyr well. I just came along to finish it for good."

The words comforted Justin and he felt better. Kara leaned over, kissed his cheek, and said that he was her hero also.

"Mandara, what was Kara's part in all of this?" asked Pectin, now feeling better and wondering where the knife wound had gone.

"Ah yes, Kara," The magician went to her. "You, my young lady, were a very important part of the ordeal. I knew that Kyr could not harm you, and if I succeeded in destroying my brother, I would lose most of my powers, and if any of our group was hurt or killed that you would be the only one to save them. If Kyr had killed me, then Justin would have needed you to imprison him again."

Kara looked puzzled, "What makes me so special to be able to do what you couldn't?"

"Kara, you are the many times removed great-grand-daughter of Kyr. As his descendant, he could not harm you, but when he hit you with his magic powers, it energized a latent power within you, one that you inherited from Kyr. He was evil, but you had the good he didn't, the good to save lives instead of taking them. The power you have will be mostly gone when my time comes to die. We now are the last of the good magicians, so we must do what we can to make our world right."

Crystal Prison of Kyr

Justin realized now why Kara had been treated differently in her village. They had been protecting her for this day.

Mandara continued, "Kara, your mother had come here with Edan on his journey to prevent Kyr from freeing himself. Edan is your father, and although your mother and Edan have wanted to be with you, they were not allowed to until you had faced Kyr. You were not allowed to know any of what would happen. That is why you were sheltered and protected by Mr. Symms. Your mother and father are anxiously awaiting your safe return in Freland."

Kara could not believe what she was hearing and was relieved that she now had an identity and a place in life. Tears were coming to her eyes and she hugged Mandara. She turned to Justin and embraced him tightly. Justin looked to Mandara and smiled.

"Do we have to go back through all your traps to get home or is your spell broken?" hoped Justin.

"No Justin, the spell is now broken and the traps are now history, but this time we will get home safe and quickly. Kara and I together have enough power to send us all back home," smiled the magician. He turned to Garth and said, "My big brave friend, you may join us in Freland as our most welcome guest, or you may return to your home. The choice is yours."

"Well, I think I will go home first and do a little bragging about my adventure, but if I'm welcome, I may join all of you at another time," laughed Garth.

"Of course, my friend, come to stay anytime," smiled Mandara.

"Mandara, what about the pyramid and Kyr?" asked Justin.

Mandara looked sadly toward the crystal monolith. "I will leave it here as a monument to the waste of life and energy that I, and my world, have suffered all these years, and as a memorial to my brother, who I will bury back into it. May he finally rest forever." Mandara took Kara's hand and then raised his free hand, speaking a strange language, waved toward the lifeless body and with that Kyr's body floated up to the apex of the pyramid and down into it. The point of the pyramid reformed sealing off the world from Kyr forever.

"Now I wish to depart this desolate place, so if everyone is ready, we will go."

Mandara called everyone together, and still holding Kara's hand, he raised his and spoke some words. The group was enveloped in a bright yellow light and vanished forever from the cold, silent Northland.

****

EPILOGUE:

Mandara and Pectin toured the world performing magic and making people happy. Garth was a hero in his land and was elected Elder. Cheek brought his mother to Freland where they lived with Justin. Justin continued his studies in agriculture and married Kara. Together, they hope to start an intensive gardening project to better feed the world. For it is now a better and safer place to raise their children.

THE END

Other books by Bob Moats

The Jim Richards Murder Novels (in order) - Classmate Murders * Vegas Showgirl Murders * Dominatrix Murders * Mistress Murders * Bridezilla Murders * Magic Murders * Strip Club Murders * Made-for-TV Murders * Mystery Cruise Murders * Talk Show Murders * Sin City Murders * Black Widow Murders * Vegas Vigilante Murders * Area 51 Murders * Mortuary Murders * Hypnotic Murders * Sunshine State Murders * Blue Suede Murders * Honky Tonk Murders * Dark Carnival Murders * Lipstick Murders * Pasta Murders * Talent Show Murders * Shyster Murders * Campground Murders * Network Murders * Reunion Murders * Big Apple Murders * Kennel Murders * Trick or Treat Murders * Santa Murders * Wiseguy Murders.
READ about Jim Richards as a young man in the novella - Marriage Can Be Murder

The Fatal Series - Fatal Rejection * Fatal Departure * Fatal Romance * Fatal Outbreak * Fatal Abduction

New! The Doyle, P.I. series - Doyle's Law * Doyle's Justice * Doyle's Quest.

www.ingramcontent.com/pod-product-compliance
Lightning Source LLC
Chambersburg PA
CBHW060631130626
46555CB00002B/754